This Gal Knows How To

The hooded man raised his knife, ~~~~~~~~ ing and moaning Dr. Potter, and started toward ~~~~~

The hidden gun in Longarm's fist was ready to shoot and wound this hooded killer, then make him talk before putting the bastard out of his misery. Only thing was, Longarm was so weak and unsteady that he didn't know if he could pull off a shot that would bring the man down without killing him.

Just as Longarm was about to fire his gun, he caught a glimpse of someone else in the doorway, and at almost the same time he heard a thundering shotgun blast. The hooded gunman was hurled straight over Longarm's bed headfirst into the window. Glass shattered as the man tumbled into the alley below. . .

The shotgun's blast had been so devastating that there was blood all over Longarm, the bed, and his wall. He knew that the hooded man was deader than a doornail.

"Who the hell *are* you!" Longarm yelled, pulling up his Colt and struggling to aim at a beautiful brunette who was dressed like a man.

"My name is Shotgun Sallie," she said, cocking back the second barrel of the big weapon and turning it on Longarm. "And, Marshal, you are just about to meet your maker."

➤ TABOR EVANS ◄

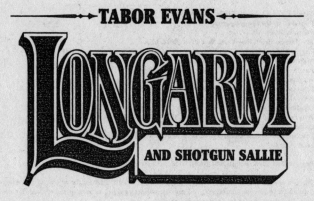

LONGARM

AND SHOTGUN SALLIE

JOVE BOOKS, NEW YORK

THE BERKLEY PUBLISHING GROUP
Published by the Penguin Group
Penguin Group (USA) Inc.
375 Hudson Street, New York, New York 10014, USA
Penguin Group (Canada), 90 Eglinton Avenue East, Suite 700, Toronto, Ontario M4P 2Y3, Canada
(a division of Pearson Penguin Canada Inc.)
Penguin Books Ltd., 80 Strand, London WC2R 0RL, England
Penguin Group Ireland, 25 St. Stephen's Green, Dublin 2, Ireland (a division of Penguin Books Ltd.)
Penguin Group (Australia), 250 Camberwell Road, Camberwell, Victoria 3124, Australia
(a division of Pearson Australia Group Pty. Ltd.)
Penguin Books India Pvt. Ltd., 11 Community Centre, Panchsheel Park, New Delhi—110 017, India
Penguin Group (NZ), 67 Apollo Drive, Rosedale, North Shore 0632, New Zealand
(a division of Pearson New Zealand Ltd.)
Penguin Books (South Africa) (Pty.) Ltd., 24 Sturdee Avenue, Rosebank, Johannesburg 2196,
South Africa

Penguin Books Ltd., Registered Offices: 80 Strand, London WC2R 0RL, England

This is a work of fiction. Names, characters, places, and incidents either are the product of the author's imagination or are used fictitiously, and any resemblance to actual persons, living or dead, business establishments, events, or locales is entirely coincidental.

LONGARM AND SHOTGUN SALLIE

A Jove Book / published by arrangement with the author

PRINTING HISTORY
Jove edition / May 2010

ISBN: 978-0-515-14795-7

JOVE®
Jove Books are published by The Berkley Publishing Group,
a division of Penguin Group (USA) Inc.,
375 Hudson Street, New York, New York 10014.
JOVE® is a registered trademark of Penguin Group (USA) Inc.
The "J" design is a trademark of Penguin Group (USA) Inc.

PRINTED IN THE UNITED STATES OF AMERICA

10 9 8 7 6 5 4 3 2 1

Chapter 1

United States Deputy Marshal Custis Long was whistling a happy tune as he strolled up Colfax Avenue on a warm Sunday morning in August. It was the time of year when you could feel that the last, glorious days of Denver's summer season were rapidly coming to an end and autumn was just around the corner. And today he was going to take the lovely, virginal Miss Lucy Coyle out for a picnic and a buggy ride . . . and maybe he'd get lucky. Longarm already had decided upon a perfect little hideaway for them to visit. It was a well-shaded and secluded glen along the South Platte River. Longarm had taken other young ladies there before and all of them had thought the setting beautiful and relaxing. So relaxing and pleasant, that they had surrendered their charms. In a wicker basket Longarm now carried two bottles of excellent French wine to put the fair lady in a loving frame of mind. Lucy was packing the sandwiches and other delicious things to eat, and the weather was promising to be perfect for this romantic outing . . . warm enough to suggest and then encourage a refreshingly naked swim in the cool creek.

Two weeks earlier Longarm had reserved the fanciest buggy available at the Drury Stables and he knew that both the horse and buggy would now be ready and waiting. The buggy's black leather would be cleaned and polished, and he had even specified a handsome black gelding as his choice of horses to rent. Before leaving town and after picking up Lucy from her church, Longarm would drive the buggy right through the center of downtown just to show the rest of the world what a fine-looking couple he and Lucy made on this perfect Sunday morning.

Longarm had had his brown suit pressed and his boots polished, and he was wearing his usual white shirt with starched collar and string tie. His snuff brown hat was cocked this morning at a slightly jaunty angle, and as he passed by the windows of storefronts, United States Deputy Marshal Custis Long was just vain enough to glance at his reflection. He'd been blessed with height, wavy brown hair, broad shoulders, and a ruggedly handsome face that most women found damned near irresistible. Still in his prime even after years of hunting down and either arresting or killing outlaws, he had his fair share of scars. Also, at the moment he was nursing a slight limp from where a pickpocket had given him a vicious kick in the shin before Longarm had cracked the man's skull with his Colt revolver.

Longarm was a block away from the stables when he noticed that a big man wearing a long black frock coat was staring at him from across the avenue and not at all in a friendly manner. Longarm kept walking, because the very last thing he wanted this morning was a confrontation. No, that would not do at all, because Lucy got out of church in about fifteen minutes and he wanted to be sitting in the buggy looking grand for their special outing.

But as Longarm passed the stranger, the man started to walk parallel to him, still on the opposite side of Colfax. And now he was staring even harder and looking very grim. Longarm's inner warning system went into high gear. He shifted the picnic basket from his right hand to his left hand, and without being obvious about it, he unbuttoned his brown tweed coat. He wore his revolver on his left hip, butt forward, and in his vest pocket he carried a cleverly hidden twin-barreled derringer in the same caliber as his six-gun.

Over his years of being a federal marshal, Longarm had necessarily made a lot of enemies, and the man who was shadowing him might well be one of those enemies, although Longarm could not identify him because he wore a hat pulled low over his face. But even without recognizing him, Longarm recognized the tenseness in his shoulders and the gun on his right hip that was tied down to his leg in the manner of professional gunfighters and outlaws.

The stable was only a block ahead and Longarm kept his eyes straight forward as he moved in a determined, long-legged stride. He rarely wore the high heels of a cowboy, much preferring to be quick on his feet and always balanced in case he needed to move fast.

The man was still moving sideways with him, but had fallen back a few paces, and Longarm found it impossible to watch him without turning his head and looking back over his shoulder.

Who is it? What does he have against me?

These were Longarm's troubled and disturbing thoughts as he neared the stable. The interior of the large barn was dim, and the moment Longarm stepped inside, he ducked back against the inner wall of the barn and gently set his picnic basket at his feet. He would wait now and see if the stranger was really serious about coming at him and why.

Longarm didn't have to wait long. Three, perhaps only two minutes passed and then he saw the shadowed outline of the man as he cautiously moved into the doorway, crouched and with a gun in his right hand.

His intention is to kill me.

Longarm drew his own pistol and decided to try to knock out the stranger if he possibly could. That way he could revive him and find out both his name and the nature of his deadly grudge.

The stranger warily entered the barn; he was big and athletically built. Longarm was in deep shadow and it all would have turned out just fine and dandy except that the stable's owner, the friendly Irishman named Mike Quinn, suddenly appeared from somewhere in the barn and said, "Your horse and buggy are ready, Marshal . . . What . . . ?"

Suddenly the stranger turned on Longarm and fired in less than a heartbeat. Fortunately, the bullet missed and Longarm slashed down with the barrel of his gun, striking his assailant on the forearm and knocking the man's pistol aside.

"Ahhh!" the man cried.

Then, before Longarm could swing the big Colt .44-40 at the stranger's skull, he sensed that a knife was coming up in the man's left hand and was aimed at his gut. Longarm jumped backward, tripped over his picnic basket, and crashed to the dirt floor. His would-be assassin dove at him with the knife, and it was all that Longarm could do to roll out of harm's way and then jump to his feet, prepared to defend his life.

"Gawdamn you, Marshal Long!" the man screamed, lunging forward with a huge Bowie knife, "I'm gonna gut you!"

"Like hell," Longarm snarled, coolly shooting his attacker in the chest.

His first bullet hardly stopped the attacker, but his second was higher and caught the man in the base of the throat, stopping him in his tracks. The man dropped his knife and lifted up on his toes, backpedaling until he struck the barn wall and began to choke and slide to the ground.

"Who in the hell are you?" Longarm shouted, knowing it was a futile question because the stranger was choking and dying. "Why were you trying to kill me?"

The attacker rattled an oath, choked on the blood that was gushing from his throat, and died.

"Holy shit!" Mike Quinn cried. "You shot him dead!"

Longarm nodded. "Yeah. He was tough and determined to kill me one way or the other. As you could see, I had no choice."

"I didn't see much because it's so dark inside this barn."

"No matter," Longarm said, kneeling down beside the dead man. "Mike, let's drag him out through the barn into the back so I can see his face in the sunlight."

"But the front is a lot closer and he looks awful heavy."

"That's true," Longarm agreed, pointing out the door. "But see those people across the street gawking at your stables? If we drag this body out in the front onto Colfax, there will be a huge crowd before you can shake a stick. I don't want that. It's a beautiful Sunday morning and I'm not going to let this dead asshole mess up my well-laid plans for today."

Quinn swallowed hard. "Whatever you say, Marshal. But you sure shot him dead, and faster than I could snap my fingers twice."

"Mike, you don't live long in my business if you're slow."

"I guess not."

Longarm snatched the man's gun from the dust of the barn floor and also his Bowie knife. "The local marshal will want these as evidence that I was attacked and he'll have the proof that the dead man shot first. Now, let's get this big bastard moving out your back door."

Mike Quinn was a small fellow, only about five foot five standing in his boots. But he was strong and so he grabbed one of the dead man's legs and, together, he and Longarm dragged the body out through the barn and into the sunlight by Mike's horse corral and outhouse.

"Roll him over," Longarm ordered. "I still haven't gotten a decent look at his face."

The Irishman did as he was told and then they stared down at the dead stranger. "Recognize him?" Quinn asked.

"Unfortunately I do not."

"But you must have met him some place and time or he wouldn't have wanted to kill you."

"You never know," Longarm mused, more to himself than to the man standing beside him with a pale face. "I have a reputation and there are a lot of men who would like to be able to say that they finally brought me down and sent me to hell. And, like you mentioned, Mike, I have a lot of personal enemies."

"But you still don't recognize him?"

Longarm removed a silk handkerchief and wiped the dead man's dirty and dusty face. Kneeling close and staring into the sightless eyes, Longarm said, "He looks kind of familiar."

"Maybe his face is on a Wanted poster over at the jail," Quinn said hopefully.

"Maybe, but I'm not taking the time to look at Wanted posters on such a fine Sunday as it is today." Longarm shook his head. "Nope, I really don't recognize the man."

"Is that good . . . or bad?" the Irishman asked.

Longarm just shrugged his shoulders in a reply. "Depends on how you want to look at this."

"I look at it as a dead man on my property, and that's not good. Not a damn bit good for my business, Marshal."

"No, I suppose not," Longarm agreed. "And I'm sorry that it had to happen in your barn. But it will draw a lot of visitors and maybe you can sell them a horse or saddle or something."

"Not too all-fired likely." Mike was looking upset and worried and Longarm wanted to offer the little Irishman some kind of comfort.

"In a few days, this will pass."

"I sure hope so."

"The thing that strikes me most," Longarm said, coming to his feet and shaking the dust from his handkerchief and then from his pants and coat, "is whoever he was, he had some real hatred for me at work deep in his craw."

"What are you going to do with him?"

"Nothing," Longarm said with an indifferent shrug. "Go get the undertaker and then visit someone at the local marshal's office and tell them what happened."

"Me!" Quinn looked shocked. "But why me?"

"Because you have a horse and buggy waiting to be rented. Or at least you had better have them ready."

"I do, but . . ."

Longarm reached for his wallet. "Mike, here is an extra dollar for all this trouble."

"I'd rather you'd keep the dollar and get the undertaker and the local officers yourself," Quinn was brave enough to say. "I don't want anything to do with this."

"It was self-defense and I haven't got the time or inclination to ruin a day with a bunch of questions and nonsense. If you go to the Heaven's Door Funeral Parlor, ask for Mr. Pincher. He's an understanding and competent fellow, though sadly lacking a sense of humor. Tell him to put this dead stranger on ice and that I'll be in tomorrow to help make arrangements for a pauper's funeral on the government's tab."

"On the government's tab?"

"That's right," Longarm said. "I killed this man in the line of duty an instant before he would have killed me because of some past lawman's duty, or maybe even because of my professional reputation. Either way, his sudden death is related to my job as a federal officer of the law and therefore the government will pay for a pauper's grave. No flowers, no fancy casket, no headstone . . . just a cross and the date of death. Mr. Pincher has done this thing several times before and he knows exactly what to do as far as the funeral arrangements."

"That's it?" Quinn asked, looking incredulous. "You're just going to waltz out of Denver and stick me with this mess?"

"I'm not going to 'waltz' anywhere, Mike." Longarm could see how upset and agitated the stableman was and he felt a sudden pang of remorse for the trouble Mike was being saddled with. "Here," he said, this time handing Mike a five-dollar gold piece. "And for your information, this shootout will make your stable very popular and might even increase your business in ways that you can't even imagine."

"And how the hell will it do that?" Mike Quinn demanded.

"Wait and see. Also, perhaps you ought to buy some ducks and chickens, then put 'em in a little cage by the front of the barn and I just bet that you'll sell 'em all! And puppies and kittens, if you can find 'em."

Mike Quinn snorted with disgust. "And you're just going to get in my buggy with my best horse and take off like no one was shot to death a few minutes ago?"

"Mike, I'm sorry," Longarm said, "but I've been angling for almost a month to get a certain lovely young lady out for the afternoon in that fancy buggy and see how my luck is running with her today."

Mike let out a string of cuss words and managed to point toward the waiting horse and buggy. Longarm went over to the horse and patted it on the neck. He admired how the horse had been curried to a shine and how the buggy was spotless and its leather seats gleamed.

"The horse and buggy looks real, real nice, Mike. First class! And if I get as lucky as I hope to get later today, I might even pass another tip your way."

"I hope you *drown*, gawdammit!"

"Aw," Longarm said, disappointed in Mike's attitude. "Don't take this incident so badly. I'll probably be back tonight, tomorrow afternoon at the latest, and you can tell the locals that's when I'll answer all their questions about the shooting."

"Thanks a whole hell of a lot!" Mike Quinn actually kicked a pile of horse turds in disgust. "Did it ever occur to you that *I* might also have plans this Sunday?"

"Of course you do! You'll go to Sweeny's Pub about noon, eat pickled eggs and drink bad beer until you can't stand up straight. Then you'll stagger back to this barn singing bawdy Irish drinking songs at the top of your lungs and then you'll pass out in your straw pile and sleep it off until Monday morning. After that you'll stagger over to Minny's Café and drink an entire pot of strong black coffee and eat a . . ."

"All right! Enough! Go away with ya!"

Mike Quinn was livid, and as Longarm got in the buggy and drove from the yard, he knew that he had exactly described the bandy little Irishman's Sunday drinking ritual and Monday morning bitter reward.

Chapter 2

Although Longarm hailed from West "By Gawd" Virginia and most of his childhood family were Baptists, he was not a churchgoing man, although he did believe. Mostly what he believed was that evil men earned their just reward both in heaven and on earth. On earth, Longarm liked to see them weep and beg for their lives before being hanged.

Now, as the Pentecostal Church that Lucy Coyle attended let out, Longarm parked the rented horse and buggy under a shady tree and watched the family men in their suits and white starched shirts and the matronly women in their Sunday dresses and hats come trooping out the front door looking quite pleased with life. There were a lot of kids, too, and all of them burst out of the church door whooping and hollering, although probably not for the Lord.

The minister, a homely young bachelor with an obvious eye on the lovely Miss Coyle, held her hand overlong and spoke earnestly into her ear. Lucy listened and then laughed and the pair hugged. It was clear to Longarm that the young minister was interested in a helluva lot more than saving Lucy's sweet soul from damnation.

"Hey!" Longarm called, stepping out from the handsome rented buggy and fine black horse. "Miss Coyle!"

When she saw Longarm, she said a quick good-bye to the disappointed minister and her other lady friends and hurried over to greet Longarm. Aware that the whole congregation was watching, Longarm gave Lucy a kiss and then scooped her up and deposited her into his rented buggy.

"Custis!" she squealed. "You can't do this in front of my church members and the Reverend Sutton! Why, you've just caused all of their tongues to start wagging and they won't stop until next Sunday."

"Oh, they'll find something else to gossip about," Longarm replied. "They remind me of a flock of hens."

"There are some fine men who regularly attend services."

"Sure there are, and I even recognize a few."

"They keep asking me when they can expect you to join them for Sunday services."

"Tell them when hell freezes over."

Lucy wasn't pleased by that answer, nor did she think it humorous. "Custis, sometimes you try me almost to distraction. I'm praying for your soul as hard as I can but I don't think it is helping even a little bit."

"Then give it up," Longarm urged. "My soul's business is between me and the Lord. And perhaps you'll be pleased to know that He and I are still on good speaking terms."

"It's a wonder, given your heathen nature."

"My nature isn't at all heathen," he protested as he climbed into the buggy, took up the reins, and set the buggy in motion. "It's just a little wilder and freer than those good men that attend your church. But I'm working on a transformation, Lucy. Honest, I am."

She looked at him closely. "Are you *really*?"

He squeezed her hand. "I know that I have my rough spots. But I'm honest and decent and awful handsome."

"Ahh!" She laughed, jabbing him in the ribs. "What you *are*, Marshal Custis Long, is conceited and arrogant!"

"Am not."

"Yes, you are."

"But no matter how you judge me, you love me all the same," he said, giving her a wink and a smile.

Lucy giggled. "You are irrepressible and a rogue."

"And handsome?"

"Yes," she admitted, shaking her head. "Devilishly handsome, and that is my problem. If you were as homely as poor Reverend Sutton, then I wouldn't give you a minute of my time."

"Your reverend looks to me like he'd sure like to give you a lot of his time and something else as well."

"Custis!" she cried in shock. "How dare you even suggest that dear Reverend Sutton has anything other than the highest regard for my soul and my spiritual welfare."

"Let's not talk about the reverend or your church, Lucy. Is our picnic lunch ready and waiting at your boarding-house?"

"It is. And you're going to love the chicken I cooked for us last night. And the apple pie and all the rest. It will take me only a few minutes to collect everything and change into a more comfortable dress. Then we'll go see that place you have been telling me about that is so pretty."

"We're going to have a wonderful day. Just you and me and not a care in the world."

"That sounds perfect."

Longarm could imagine that by now there was a big crowd out in front of the Drury Stables and that the local

constable would be damned upset that Longarm wasn't
there to answer all his silly questions. But why ruin this day
going over and over the shooting? The town marshal's
questions would be the same as they always were after a
shooting: Do you know the man you killed? Why was he
trying to kill you? Who shot first? And on and on as the
man scribbled into his little notepad and then asked Longarm to come in and sign a statement, putting his words
down for posterity. There would, of course, also be the
newspaper reporters and others seeking to suck out the last
bit of gory detail and sensationalism about this latest of
Longarm's shootouts.

To hell with all that, he thought, pulling up before Lucy's
boardinghouse and helping her down from the buggy. *I
would rather skinny dip and make passionate love to Miss
Lucy Coyle.*

It was nearly one o'clock in the afternoon when they reached
the little bend in the river where the grass was lush and you
could picnic beside the water without worrying about being
seen. The cottonwoods hung low over the river and there
were lots of birds and willows. Longarm knew that you
could wade out into the river and that it would be cool and
refreshing on a warmish day such as this.

Longarm pulled the buggy to a halt. "Well," he asked,
"isn't this spot as pretty as I promised you?"

"Yes, it's a lovely spot to have a Sunday picnic."

"No one ever comes here," Longarm promised. "I guess
they stop at places along the river closer to town. But I am
convinced that coming a little farther is worth the time and
effort."

"Absolutely," she said jumping down from the buggy before Longarm could come around and help her. Lucy

scooped up the picnic basket and almost skipped over to the riverside. "The water looks inviting and the current doesn't appear to be at all swift."

"It's a safe place to swim. There's a deep, fast current out in the middle, but near shore it's warm and gentle."

"Get us that blanket, please."

Longarm got the blanket and Lucy told him where to spread it near the water's edge. Then she unpacked their picnic basket while Longarm unhitched and hobbled the horse so it could also enjoy the day eating the lush meadow grass.

"Custis, our food is ready!"

Longarm hurried over and sat beside Lucy and soon they were helping themselves to the chicken and other delicious things to eat. "Where did you learn to cook chicken this delicious?" Longarm asked.

"My mother was an excellent cook. She taught me at an early age." She laughed. "I can also sew and mend. I'm a good homemaker, Custis. I'll make someone a wonderful wife."

Longarm knew that she was staring at him, waiting for a response, but instead he reached for a drumstick and said, "Fine day to be alive and with someone as pretty as you, Lucy."

"Thank you," she replied, unable to hide the disappointment from her voice.

When they finished their picnic, Lucy and Longarm stretched out on the blanket and gazed up at the big white clouds pushing east from over the Rocky Mountains. Birds sang in the cottonwoods and willows and a muskrat splashed in the water somewhere along the bank.

"What are you thinking about right now?" Longarm asked.

"I was wondering how it would feel if we could freeze this perfect spot and perfect day in time."

Longarm frowned. "You mean be stuck like this forever?"

"Sort of. Wouldn't that be lovely?"

"Might get a little boring," he offered, and then quickly added, "but then again it could hardly get any nicer."

"No, it couldn't."

Longarm rolled over on his side and kissed Lucy. He seriously kissed her sweet lips and brought her up tight against himself. When she kissed him right back with passion, his lips traveled down her neck. He sucked on her earlobe and that seemed to excite her tremendously because she started breathing fast and squirming with desire.

Pulling away for a moment, Longarm said, "This is just what I was hoping for, Lucy. But lying out here in the sun is a little warmish."

"Do you want to move our blanket into the shade of these big cottonwood trees?"

"I was thinking of going for a swim . . . or at least sitting in the water and letting it cool down our bodies."

"I didn't expect that a man with your reputation would want to 'cool down' a woman's body."

Longarm blushed and suspected that he was being teased. "Well, I was thinking of how good that water would feel on a warm day like this."

"But I didn't bring a bathing suit."

"Dang," he said, trying to feign disappointment. "Neither did I. I guess we'll have to shuck out of our clothes and go for a skinny dip."

Lucy's eyes widened. "Custis! What do you take me for?"

"A lady."

"Well, a lady does not go swimming nude with a man who is not her husband."

"Oh," he replied, "that's not altogether true."

"Well, it is for me!"

Longarm decided it was time for some help from the wine. He popped a cork and poured them two full glasses. "A toast to us, Lucy! And to many more happy outings like today."

"I'll drink to that."

Longarm knew Lucy loved champagne and he was going to give her more than her fill. "And to your *rare* beauty," he said, topping off her glass.

Lucy actually blushed. He could see a glaze of perspiration on her face and he expected she was getting quite warm as the sun beat down on them with late-afternoon intensity.

"And to us," she said. "And perhaps . . . perhaps someday a wedding?"

Longarm damned near choked but then quickly managed to grin and raise his glass. "Drink up!" he urged. "There's a second bottle in the buggy."

"*Two* bottles?" she asked, eyebrows raised.

"Sure! I knew it would be hot out here today, and since you don't want to go cool down in the river, we're going to have to keep drinking. You see, when you sweat you have to drink more."

"I thought you were supposed to drink *water* when you sweat and are too warm."

"Well, we haven't got any water, Lucy. Not unless you want to drink out of the river."

"I do not."

"Then we'll just have to settle for the two bottles of champagne."

Lucy thought about that for a few minutes while she looked around and sipped from her glass. She found a silk handkerchief and dabbed the beads of sweat from her brow, then she used it to fan herself. "Are you *sure* no one comes around here?"

"I'm absolutely sure."

"Well, perhaps if we kept our bodies under the surface of the cool water then we . . ."

"Great idea!" he said, grabbing her hand and pulling Lucy to her feet. "Let's shuck our clothes and jump right in so we can cool down. Have you ever been naked in running water?"

She tried to seem a bit offended by his question. "Why, of course not!"

"Then you're in for a real treat because you'll just love the way the cool water feels moving past your hot skin."

Lucy drained her glass. "Custis, are you certain that no fish or anything will bite or nibble at my naked body?"

"Naw!"

"What about beavers? They have those huge front teeth, don't they?"

"Sure, but they like wood, not people. If there are any beavers around, they'll be working on a dam or something and they disappear the minute they see you."

"Any water snakes?"

"Nope."

She fanned her face with her hand and looked anxiously up and down the river. Seeing nothing, she finally said, "Turn around, Custis, and you must promise me that you won't peek."

"I'm a *gentleman*, Lucy. Of course I'm not going to peek."

"And neither will I. We'll just . . . just avert our eyes until we are up to our necks in the river."

"Sounds like the right thing to do," he said, nearly choking on the ridiculous lie. "But let's polish off this bottle of champagne and take our glasses and the second bottle out into the water. We can sit on our rumps . . . with the river up to our necks, mind you . . . and enjoy the second bottle."

"Well, I don't . . ."

"You'll love it."

"Have you done this before with a woman?" she asked.

"You're the first, Lucy."

"I honestly doubt that, Custis. Things are moving very fast for us today and you seem pretty experienced in this sort of thing."

"I just don't want you fainting because it's so warm," he said. "And I think you're really going to like sitting in that cold water."

"All right."

Longarm was out of his clothes in minutes, leaving his gun and belt as well as his badge on the blanket. He upended the first bottle of champagne, draining it dry, then grabbed crystal glasses and the second bottle and placed them carefully on a flat river rock. Finally, he dove into the water and came up shouting, "Lucy, this feels wonderful!"

"Keep your eyes on the other side of the river," she said. "You promised."

"Sure did. Come on, Lucy!"

He heard her wade into the slow-moving river just a few yards away. Heard her gasp with either shock or delight, and then heard a splash.

"Can I look now?"

"I suppose so."

She was swimming in water that could not have been more than four feet deep, and even though the river was not clear, Longarm could still see the pale shape of her lovely body. And she was laughing. Really, really laughing.

"This is *fun!*" she called. "And you're right; the moving water feels wonderful and refreshing on a hot day like this."

"I knew you'd like it."

Longarm waded out to stand close as she frolicked around him like a little girl, laughing and splashing water in his direction.

"Oh, Custis, this is simply divine!"

Longarm moved over to grab her hand and he stood her up. "And you haven't seen the half of it yet, honey."

He took her into his arms and held her cool, wet body tightly against his own body. Then he began kissing her, and this time his lips moved to her cool and luscious breasts.

"Custis, please stop."

She didn't sound all that determined to make him stop so he kept kissing her breasts and then he sucked on her nipples, the right one first and then the left. Lucy's breath was coming faster than a racing train, and when Longarm's manhood poked at her she wrapped herself around him like a vine on a tree, and the next thing they knew he was inside of her and they were doing it in the current. Unfortunately, Longarm stepped on a submerged mossy rock and tumbled over sideways. For a moment, Longarm thought he might have ruined the mood, but apparently not because Lucy grabbed his tool and brought it back inside of her. He then carried her over to the riverbank and took her right there in the slick, brown mud, both of them going wild with desire.

"Oh my gawd! I can't believe what we've done out here

under the open sky," he said when at last he emptied his seed and rolled off into the mud.

Longarm took her hand. "It wasn't your first time, was it, Lucy."

"No," she admitted. "But I've had almost no experience. And never out of doors in the water."

"Then in a way, I am the first."

"Yes, you are, Custis." Lucy pushed herself out into the river. "I'm a muddy mess!"

"So am I."

He followed her out into water until it was up to his chest and then they washed each other off in the current. "Are you having a good time?"

"I'll never forget today," she told him. "Not if I live to be a hundred. Not even if we never get married."

"I'm just not the marrying kind," he told her.

"I know. But people change. Maybe you've already changed just in the last hour. Would that be so impossible?"

He couldn't bear to tell her the truth. "No, Lucy, it is not impossible."

She hugged his neck and clung to him. "You will never meet another woman that would be as good a wife to you as I would be."

"I can believe that."

"Then will you at least stay open to the possibility?"

"Why don't we get out of this water and go lie down on the blanket to dry off and make love again?"

"Would that help you move toward a decision to marry me someday?"

"I think it might," he told her in truthfulness.

"Then I'm all for it!"

Longarm carried Lucy out of the water and up onto the blanket. He kissed her gently and they talked about the weather and about nothing at all. Then, feeling aroused by the hot afternoon sun, he mounted her again, this time taking her even more forcefully. Lucy was a lioness and she wrapped her legs around his waist and would not unlock them until she had satisfied not only Longarm, but also herself.

When they finished they were both sweating profusely and went back into the river to cool down.

"I never want this day to end," she sighed, hugging him tightly.

"Me neither," he said. "In fact . . ."

Whatever words Longarm was about to say next died on his lips as he stood in the river holding Lucy and watching five hooded horsemen emerge from the cottonwoods with rifles in their fists.

Longarm was naked and absolutely helpless. The sun was directly in his eyes so he couldn't even see the faces of the killers. But he did see the sunlight glancing off their buckles and weapons as the five men took their casual aim. In the split second before their rifles thundered, Longarm twisted violently and drove both him and Lucy underwater.

His only thought was to stay submerged and attempt to reach the deep and swift middle current. Even if he managed to do that, Longarm figured the South Platte River would finish the job that the five men on horseback had started and that, either way, he and Lucy were as good as dead.

Chapter 3

Longarm was being twisted and spun by the river as he tried to hang on to Lucy Coyle and at the same time move deeper into the current. He had no idea who the horsemen were, nor did he really care at this desperate moment. All his power and concentration was focused on staying underwater and hanging on to Lucy, keeping them both alive as they were whirled downriver.

Suddenly he struck a submerged tree and pain shot through the entire length of his body as its sharp branches ripped his body and tore Lucy from his grasp. The pain was so intense that Longarm nearly gagged, and he fought to the surface knowing that he was badly wounded.

"Lucy!"

She was very close to him, but in the instant before he could reach out to grab the woman, more rifle shots crashed across the river's roiling surface. Longarm saw blood, brain, and bone explode from the top of Lucy's head just before she disappeared. He dove for her knowing the woman was already dead. Groping in the fast water, he momentarily felt his grasping fingers entangle themselves in her hair and then she was gone.

Longarm slammed into a boulder and felt madness and death overcoming his reason. Moments later he struck some other submerged object, tumbled over and over and blindly fought to reach the surface for air. When his head burst above the water, more shots followed and Longarm saw the five horsemen racing along the riverbank, trying to tear through the tangle of fallen trees and brush to keep abreast of him. Their hoods were now gone but everything was moving so fast that he had no time to recognize their faces. All he knew for certain was that Lucy was dead, her nude body being carried downriver toward Denver, and that he was somehow still alive.

Longarm glanced up at the dying sun, took a deep breath, and let the Platte carry him along. He felt the river bend and knew that at the rate he was being carried, he would be on the outskirts of Denver within a few hours if he was not shot or drowned.

Over and over Longarm kept resurfacing, grabbing a quick breath of fresh air and then diving. He struck several other sunken logs and knew that his flesh was being shredded from his lean frame. He was not at all certain he could endure the river much longer and knew for sure that he could not survive the men who were out to see him dead.

Darkness had at last fallen as the river still bore Longarm along. Weak and shivering, keeping only his face above water, he finally managed to swim out of the current's strong grip and strike for a cove overgrown with reeds. When his hands and knees touched mud, he paddled weakly into the hidden seclusion of the reeds and lay panting and shivering uncontrollably.

"He's got to be here someplace! Keep looking!" someone shouted from upriver.

"Maybe we hit him, or more likely he drowned!" came a voice from not far downriver.

"I want to see that sonofabitch's body!"

"But it's getting too dark!"

"Gawdamn you, keep searching *both* sides of the river."

Longarm tried to focus on the voices. He wanted to burn the sound of them forever into his exhausted mind. He wanted to hear those voices when he stood before their owners and emptied his gun into their guts.

Someday. Somewhere. Somehow.

"I found the woman's body!" came an excited voice in the falling light. "She's over here tangled up in a tree's roots."

Longarm heard the splashing of running horses in shallow water, followed by, "Damn, she sure had a fine body! What a rotten shame we weren't able to take her alive and rape her all night."

"Yeah, if the top of her head wasn't half blown off and she wasn't so muddy, why, I'd drop my pants and give it to her body right now."

"Sick bastard!"

There was coarse laughter and then, "Keep looking for the marshal. He's probably dead, but I want to make damned sure of it."

"Oh, he's dead all right. But at least he got to screw that woman before we sent him to hell."

"Lucky bastard."

"*Dead* bastard is more like it!"

Longarm heard all this and more. And while he listened

a cold, hard hatred started building in his torn and bloodied body. He racked his brain trying to remember if he had ever heard those voices before. But as hard as he tried, he could not recall them. No matter. He would live and he would get his revenge if it was the last thing he did in this world. Lucy Coyle had been a beautiful woman, inside and out. She had wanted him to marry her and instead he'd gotten her killed. She hadn't deserved to die . . . not like this and not in any other unspeakably horrible way. If the truth were told about them making love and swimming in the nude, Longarm knew that Lucy Coyle would be looked down upon and joked about, and her decent Christian reputation forever tarnished and destroyed.

Longarm decided that before he even thought about taking care of his own physical needs he would find Lucy and carry her back to their picnic spot. He would wash and dress her body and then he'd comb what was left of her hair and he'd take her directly to a mortuary where a friend of his worked and tell that good man that no one was to see her defiled body before it was buried.

And there would be more questions for the local town marshal. Many more questions, none of which he wanted to answer because this was a matter of a lady's honor. He would only say that they had been picnicking and were ambushed by five unknown and hooded horsemen. He would not tell a soul that he and Miss Coyle had made wild love . . . not once, but twice . . . and swam like little kids in the cool river, laughing as if life would never end.

Longarm knew with a deep sadness and inner-core sickness that he had failed Lucy Coyle in life, and he'd be damned if he'd fail her a second time after her death. He would uphold her name and her honor, and when he was able to, he'd track those five horsemen down, even if that meant going to the very ends of this earth.

The stars came out one by one and the hot summer day cooled down quickly with the night. Longarm had limped out of the river and hobbled over sharp sticks and stones as he trod cautiously along the riverbank until he saw Lucy hanging on naked branches just off the riverbank. Moonlight did her a kindness, and he waded out into the water and collected her body, sobbing unashamedly.

"I'll make 'em pay for this, Lucy! I swear that I will if it takes the rest of my life!"

Longarm lifted her broken and impaled body from the tree branches and carried her out of the river. He began walking back toward where they'd picnicked and made love.

Unarmed and naked, he was bleeding from a dozen or more cuts and gashes, and feeling both weak and unsteady as he carried Lucy, vowing never to stumble and let her fall.

Their picnic basket had been smashed, their blanket shat and pissed upon as a final humiliation. Longarm kicked the defiled blanket into the river, found his clothes, and dressed. His gun and badge were missing, which came as no surprise. Their rented buggy had been shot up, and the fine rented gelding was nowhere to be found.

Longarm bathed Lucy's body and carefully dressed it. He laid Lucy out on the grass under the moonlight and tried to understand how something so good had come to such a tragic ending. He couldn't for the life of him understand why he had not been killed instead of Lucy Coyle, and supposed that the bullet that had struck her head was intended for his own. She had not been the real target, although if they had killed him, she would most certainly have died at their hands as well.

Shaky and weak, once dressed, he pulled on his boots, crammed his hat down tight over his head, and started walking back toward Denver. If he didn't pass out from loss of blood or run into the five killers, he figured he could be in town before daylight. First he would find the mortician and ask him to come and collect Lucy and keep her out of the sight of curious eyes. Then he would head to the doctor for himself to bandage his body, and afterward ... afterward he supposed he'd have to visit the town marshal and make his report.

But what could he tell the local constable? How could he explain what had happened to him? And how could he face his own boss and coworkers at the federal marshal's office. His boss and his friend, Billy Vail, would of course be sympathetic and do everything in his power to catch the five killers. But Longarm didn't even have descriptions of the men to give Vail or anyone else so, realistically, what could be done?

Five men had taken target practice and their bloody revenge. It now occurred to Longarm that one of them had been riding a pinto and another was mounted on a bald-faced buckskin. Those colors were not all that common and they might just be enough to lead him to the vicious and cold-blooded killers.

"I'll shoot them down to the very last man or die trying," he vowed as he staggered on toward the growing lights of Denver.

Chapter 4

Longarm lay stretched bare-assed naked on the doctor's examination table. The man bent over him, suturing up the last of his deep wounds, was Doctor Edward J. Potter, a longtime friend and the best sawbones in Denver. Over the previous years he'd dug numerous bullets out of Longarm and saved his life twice.

"Custis," Doc said, his expression grim, "I've probably seen you in worse physical shape, but I can't recall when. If you told me that a grizzly bear had attacked you, I wouldn't be in the least bit surprised. There's hardly a place on your body that isn't cut, scraped, bruised, or gouged. And some of these wounds are especially deep and dirty. I've done what I can to clean them out, then sew and bandage them up, but you've lost a lot of blood and I'm worried about infection."

"Doc, is there any other good news you want to tell me?" Longarm asked cryptically. "Or does that about cover it?"

Doc Potter shook his head. "You must be like a cat with nine lives . . . but, dammit, when I look at all the scars you carry and think about all the times I've had you on this table, I'm ready to believe that you've definitely used all nine of 'em up."

"Look, Doc, I know you're frustrated but you have to remember that I was having a nice Sunday picnic with a wonderful young woman," Longarm replied. "I didn't go looking for trouble. Yesterday along the South Platte River getting into trouble was the last thing on my mind."

"Do you realize that this entire town is up in arms about what happened out there with you and Miss Coyle? Her minister, Reverend Sutton, has been raising Cain and he's even gone to the newspaper to put in a story against you. He says that you alone are responsible for Miss Coyle's death and he wants your head served on his altar."

"Well, he won't get it," Longarm said in a steely voice. "But he's right about me being responsible. If Miss Coyle hadn't gone on that picnic with me she'd still be alive. I hold myself completely responsible for her death, and it's a burden I'll carry for the rest of my days."

The doctor finished tying off the last suture and then he threw his forceps on a tray and glared at Longarm. "Which, I might add, could be damned few. If five men tried to kill you, I imagine they were pretty serious. The local marshal, Oscar Duncan, is madder'n a wet hen. He says first you gun down a man at the Drury Stables yesterday, then you rent a buggy, and the next thing he knows, Miss Coyle is dead."

"It was a hard, hard weekend, Doc. But Mike Quinn was a witness to the shooting at his stables. He saw that I was just defending my life and had to kill that stranger in self-defense. And yesterday out on the Platte, well, I just don't yet know who those five horsemen were or why they were after me."

"And you didn't even see their faces?"

"Nope. When they first appeared they were wearing hoods and in shadow of the trees. Later, when I was fighting for my life in the river and trying to help Miss Lucy, my eyes were full of water and things were moving so fast I couldn't clearly see their faces. Everything was a blur."

"That river just about tore you apart, Custis. You must have struck every submerged snag and boulder. You've got some cracked ribs, and that deep wound in your chest ought to have killed you outright. My guess is it's not more than an inch from your heart. Dammit, man, I had to dig *wood* out of your chest!"

"And I'm sure you'll give me a hefty bill for your excellent services, Doc. But what am I supposed to tell you or anyone else? We were set upon and had no choice but to jump into the river and try to escape."

Doc Potter wasn't buying that line. "Rumor is that neither your clothes nor those of Miss Coyle were dirty or torn up like they ought to be had you jumped into the water."

"Don't know what to say about that, but I sure wish people didn't have such filthy minds and wagging tongues."

"Well, most do," Doc snapped. "And it doesn't matter to me what you and Miss Coyle were doing when the ambushers appeared. What I *do* know is that I've never seen you unarmed, and so I assume that you were swimming when you were attacked."

"Assume any damn thing you want, Doc. I'm sticking with my story because I owe that much to the memory of Lucy Coyle."

"That is commendable and understandable because you are an honorable man and Miss Coyle was a lady. But the Reverend Sutton is telling his congregation that you are the devil incarnate and you aren't fit to wear a lawman's badge. That you have a virgin's innocent blood on your hands and ought to stand trial for the murder of that young woman."

"The reverend was in love with Miss Coyle and he's talking crazy talk," Longarm said. "Can I get dressed now?"

"Sure. But I'm warning you to go to your apartment and rest for at least a week."

"We both know that I can't do that."

"If you don't," Doc Potter warned, "you could lose your health. And I'm dead serious. You're weak and that's when infections attack. You've got to build your blood back up or you could wind up with a permanent loss of your health and maybe even your life."

"I'll take it easy," Longarm promised, knowing he would do no such thing.

There was a loud knock on the door and the doctor turned and shouted, "I'm examining my patient!"

"I need to talk to Custis Long right now!"

"It's Marshal Duncan," the doctor said with obvious exasperation. "He's really up in arms."

"Let him in," Longarm told the doctor. "I might as well get the rest of this bad business put behind me."

"I'll be in my little office next door," the doctor said. "If you allow Marshal Duncan to seriously upset you, then some of the wounds might start to bleed because your heart will be pumping faster and harder. So I'm going to insist that Marshal Duncan mind his manners and I won't let him harass you for more than five minutes."

"I can handle Duncan," Longarm said. "And, Doc, thanks for the help. You've done an outstanding job, as usual."

Doctor Potter hesitated at the door to his small surgical room. "Custis, when I was a medical student in Boston, it would have been interesting to study your body in our anatomy laboratory because it is such a remarkable example of how the human body can somehow survive multiple trauma and still function. You are a walking bundle of scar tissue and I'm quite serious when I say that all these injuries will ultimately take their toll on your health and vitality."

"Thanks again, Doc. Let Marshal Duncan in."

"Maybe I should stay here with you," Potter suggested. "I know that you two have never liked each other, and these deaths have probably sent Marshal Duncan right over the edge."

"I'll be fine. Go see some other patients."

"I'll visit you this evening at your apartment. I want to make sure that the sutures I put in are holding, and there are a few dressings that will need my attention and changing."

"I'll look forward to your call and I promise to have a bottle of my best whiskey available."

Doctor Potter opened the door, which was immediately filled with a big, heavyset man wearing a shiny badge on his broad chest. Marshal Oscar Duncan was about six foot tall and weighed at least two-hundred and fifty pounds. Red-faced and overweight, he had a loud, blustery voice and was physically intimidating. He was a bully behind a badge and proud of it.

"Gawdamn you, Custis Long!" he bellowed. "What are you trying to do to me and my office! First you gun down a man in the stable and leave before I can take your statement, then you go off with a fine girl and get her shot to death by the river!"

"Tone it down, Duncan," Longarm warned as he painfully eased into his clothing. "I'm not in a mood to be badgered or yelled at. I've had all the trouble I can about stand right now and my fuse is burnin' damn short."

"I don't give a shit about your fuse or your feelings! I've got not one but *two* murders, and you're the cause of 'em both. And so far I don't have a statement or a single gaw-damn clue as to what is going on."

"I had to kill that man at Drury Stables in self-defense and Mike Quinn is my witness to that fact. I told him to give you a statement and to tell you that I'd come into your office and give you my statement on Monday."

"Yeah. Yeah. He told me that, only I don't accept state-ments from witnesses when the culprit is the one I want to talk to."

"I'm a 'culprit'?" Longarm asked, raising his eyebrows. "A culprit to what?"

"You're the one that shot that man! And don't get wise with me, mister federal marshal. I may not make as much money as you or have your damned killer's reputation, but I'm the real law in Denver, not you and not your boss or any of those other federal sonsofbitches that sit around scratching their fat asses all day while shuffling paperwork in the United States Federal Building!"

Longarm had had just about enough. "Marshal Duncan, if you don't lower your voice and mind your manners, I'm going to come off this table and whip you down to a nub-bin."

"You couldn't whip a puppy dog given the shape you're in. Have you looked at yourself in a mirror lately?"

Longarm buckled on his belt and knotted his fists. He was just about to take a swing at Duncan when Doc Potter burst back into the room and got between him and the marshal.

"Hold on here!" Dr. Potter shouted. "You're both lawmen and yet you're about to fight! Oscar, what the hell is the matter with you? Can't you see that Custis is in terrible shape?"

"He's in good enough shape to threaten me, and I'm sick of his making my job and my life miserable."

"I think," Doc Potter said, "it is time that you left my office. I can see that you are in no state of mind to interview Custis, and I believe it would be in everyone's best interest if we let things cool down for a few hours."

"I don't have a few hours!" Marshal Duncan swore. "If what I heard is correct, five horsemen opened fire on Miss Coyle and this federal asshole. Miss Coyle is dead. I got another dead man over at the Heaven's Door Funeral Parlor and no one even knows his damned name. So, Doc, I need some answers from Custis Long, and I need them right now!"

"If you don't stop shouting at me," Longarm warned, "all you're going to get is a fist in the face and a thorough ass kicking."

At those words, Denver Marshal Oscar Duncan went into a complete rage and it was all that Doc Potter could do to shove the big lawman out of his office.

"Nice work, Custis," Potter said, panting and looking furious. "You and Duncan sure set fine examples."

Longarm grabbed his shirt and started to button it. "Take it easy, Doc, or you'll bust a gasket, and then who would I have to patch me up the next time I get into a fix?"

"I don't know why I bother saving you time after time."

"Could it possibly be because I actually pay you for your services?"

Potter sighed with resignation. "Custis, I've got an office back door, and when you're fully dressed I suggest you use it and avoid Marshal Duncan on your way out. And I have another suggestion."

"I know. Take it easy for a week."

"Yes, and lock your door and keep your gun close at hand," Potter warned. "If five men are after you, the odds are that they won't come in a bunch but will keep after you until the job is done."

"I'm not waiting for them to come calling, Doc. My plan is to go right after them. Force the trouble on my own terms."

"If you were smart . . . really smart . . . you'd leave town under cover and stay gone for a month. You'd rest and re-cuperate and simply wait while things simmer down and maybe those five men will get tired of hunting for you and go far, far away."

"You know I could never do that, given what they did to Miss Lucy. I'm going to kill them all, Doc. I'm going to make them pay by dying hard."

"Sounds like revenge to me. Not the law."

"Then it sounds exactly right, because I'm going to give up my badge and take the law into my own hands. In my mind, Doc, those five have already been tried and convicted of murder in the first degree. And they won't even get the benefit of final rites before they die because I'll be their judge, jury, and executioner all rolled into one."

"You're going to give up your federal officer's badge?"

Longarm nodded, his lips pressed tightly together.

"I'm very sorry to hear that."

"So am I," Longarm told the man. "But when I start hunting those men I want no boundaries or limitations placed on my actions. No rules or laws or anyone telling me about legal justice. All I want is their *blood*!"

Doc Potter opened his mouth to try to change Longarm's mind, but he saw the lawman's grim, battered, and torn face and knew he'd be wasting his breath. So he clamped his jaw shut, turned around, and went out the door to see his other waiting patients.

Chapter 5

Longarm was feverish and dozing on his bed fully clothed when he was roused by a knock on his door. Head spinning and feeling woozy, he weakly called out, "Who is it?"

"Doc Potter. Open up."

Summoning all of his remaining strength, Longarm pushed himself off the bed and weaved his way to the door, which he unlocked. "Come in, Doc. Whiskey is on the kitchen table."

The moment that Dr. Potter entered he could see the feverish color of Longarm's skin and the slightly glazed look to his eyes. "My gawd, man!" he said, putting the back of his hand to Longarm's forehead. "You're burning up with fever!"

"I'm not feeling all that great."

Doc put his arm around Longarm's waist and led him back to his bed. "How long have you been feverish?"

"Almost from the time I left your office."

"We've got to get your temperature down," the doctor said. "You need to drink a lot of water, and I'm going to rush down to the saloon for ice."

"I'll be all right."

"You'll be out of your mind if that fever elevates any more." Doc opened his medical kit and found a thermometer. "Here, open wide."

A moment later, Doc stared at the thermometer. "It's 106 degrees! That's bad, Custis. Real bad." He reached for a pitcher beside Longarm's bed and found it empty. "I'll get ice and plenty of water right now. You need to help me get this temperature under control."

"It'll run its course in due time."

"Don't tell me what it will do! *I'm* the doctor, not you. A temperature this high can affect your brain and even kill you."

Longarm winked up at the physician. "Do tell?"

"I'm going to get that ice and water and be right back!" Doc called. "I'll lock this door on my way out."

"You can't, Doc. Only locks from the inside." Longarm tried to get off the bed and failed. He simply had no strength and he was on fire.

"I'll be back in less than five minutes."

"Don't bust a gasket, Doc. I need you."

"You sure do."

Doc raced out of the room slamming the door in his wake. Longarm heard the pounding of his footsteps down the hallway and then the stairs. Doc Potter was a good friend indeed and he worried more than necessary. Longarm had felt worse than this in his lifetime, he just couldn't exactly remember when. Closing his eyes, he reached out blindly for his almost new gun and holster hanging close by on his bedpost. He unholstered the gun and slipped it in his bed. He had always kept that identical backup rig hidden, and he was damned glad of it because one of the ambushers out by the Platte had stolen his regular .44-40 Colt revolver. And then, too, there was the hideout derringer attached to his watch fob that he also had still in his possession, and finally there was a loaded Winchester in his clothes closet. The trouble was that Longarm knew that he couldn't get up and walk to his closet now even if his very life depended upon it.

Longarm dozed off and was awakened by Doc's return. "Here," the physician said, cradling Longarm's head in one hand and holding out a glass of water. "Drink it all down."

"Yes, sir."

Longarm managed to choke the water down and Doc immediately refilled the glass. "Drink another. Before I'm done, you're going to drink this whole pitcher of water."

"Then I'll be pissin' like a horse."

"That's right," Doc told him.

"How about the ice?"

"I've got it ready. Drink one more glass and I'll put some ice on your head and chest."

"That's gonna feel real good, Doc."

"I'm sure that it will."

For the next two hours, Dr. Edward J. Potter poured water down Longarm's gullet and rubbed his body with ice. Every twenty minutes or so he would pull out the thermometer and jam it under Longarm's tongue. "Temperature is finally going down," Doc announced with relief. "It's 102 degrees. How do you feel now?"

"Like dog shit."

Potter actually smiled. "At least your bad sense of humor is returning to normal."

"Doc, I'm sick of water. How about we have a little whiskey and then you help me out of this bed? I've got a chamber pot underneath it and I really need to take a piss."

"Small wonder. We've gone through three pitchers of water."

"We have? I don't recall you going out for the second and third pitcher."

"I didn't. I asked the bartender to send someone up with refills."

"Oh, I see."

"One more refill is coming and then I think I can safely leave you and go home to my own wife and bed."

"You ought to do that, Doc. Molly is a fine woman and she's probably worried sick about you being gone."

"She's used to my house calls and long hours away both day and night. Molly won't worry unless I don't turn up for another twelve hours."

"Good."

There was a knock on the door. "That will be the boy from the saloon with more water," Doc announced, getting up and heading over to unlock the door.

But when he opened it, a man wearing a black hood and with a gun in his hand was standing in wait. Before Doc could even think about slamming the door in his face, the hooded man bullied his way inside the apartment and pistol-whipped Dr. Potter across the side of his head, sending him crashing to the floor.

Longarm blinked and stared at the hooded man, who said, "We figured that if you were alive you'd be in bad shape. Looks like you are and so is your doctor."

"Sooner or later I'm gonna get even with you," Longarm vowed.

"Ha! You're gonna die in your bed and the only question in my mind is if I need to also kill the doctor."

"You don't," Longarm told the assassin. "He couldn't see your face so there's no need to do that. No need at all."

"Ah, but he's your friend, isn't he?"

"Nope. I never liked the man but he's a good doctor and he works cheap."

"Maybe I'll let him live."

"Why not?" Longarm asked, fingers slipping around the hidden Colt resting right by his side. "But here's another thing you should think about before you pull that trigger."

"And that would be?"

"People will hear the gunshot. They'll come racing in here and then you'll be trapped and caught."

"I figure I can kill anyone who gets in my way."

"Maybe. But maybe not."

The hooded man thought about that for a minute, his finger tightening on his trigger. Then he relaxed, holstered the gun, and drew a large knife from his belt. "I'll tell you what, Custis Long. Rather than shoot you, I'll take more pleasure in cutting off your balls and then slitting your throat. How does that sound?"

"Sounds pretty bad," Longarm told the man. "But before you do your cutting, I'd sure like to know who you and the others are and why you're all so intent on killing me."

"Yeah, I'll bet you are curious about that."

"Knowing who you are and why this is happening would be my last and only request."

"I don't give a damn about satisfying your request!" The hooded man raised his knife, stepped over the bleeding and moaning Dr. Potter, and started toward Longarm.

The hidden gun in Longarm's fist was ready and he had already decided that he would do his very best to shoot and wound this hooded killer and then make him talk before putting the bastard out of his misery. Only thing was, Longarm was so weak and unsteady that he didn't know if he could pull off an accurate shot that would bring the man down without killing him.

Just as Longarm was about to draw and fire his gun, he caught a glimpse of someone else in the doorway and almost at the same time he heard a thundering shotgun blast. The hooded gunman was hurled straight over Longarm's bed and went headfirst into the window. Glass shattered as the man tumbled out of the second story apartment and into the alley below, knocking over garbage cans when he landed.

The shotgun's blast had been so devastating that there was blood all over Longarm, the bed, and his wall. He knew that the hooded man was deader than a doornail.

"Who the hell *are* you!" Longarm yelled, pulling up his Colt and struggling to aim at a beautiful brunette dressed like a man.

"My name is Shotgun Sallie," she said, cocking back the second barrel of the big weapon and turning it on Longarm. "And, Marshal, you are just about to meet your maker."

"No!" Doc groaned as he struggled to get off the floor. "Don't do it!"

For just an instant, the woman's eyes hardened like obsidian and then she dropped her glance toward the prostrated physician. "If I blow Marshal Custis Long all to hell, I guess I'll have to kill you as well," she said matter-of-factly. "And that would be a pity because Colorado is lacking in good doctors."

"Please don't kill us," Doc Potter begged. "You just killed one of the men responsible for the death of Miss Lucy Coyle."

"Yeah," the woman said, her smoking gun barrel still trained on Longarm. "But from what I've been told, the main one responsible for my sister's death is lying right there in that bed, and I mean to put an end to his life!"

"I'm sorry," Longarm said, dropping his pistol to his side. "I . . . loved your sister. I really did. I was even thinking about marrying Lucy."

"Bullshit!"

"Well," Longarm confessed, "not right away or anything. But I loved her and I know that she loved me."

"You got her *killed*, you badge-toting sonofabitch!"

"I'm sorry, and I swear I'll get revenge if you don't blow a hole in me like you just did that man you sent through my window."

"I'm glad I killed him and I'll be even gladder after I kill *you*!"

Longarm saw her finger tightening on the trigger and he knew he was a goner. But just then, Doc Potter threw out his arm in wild desperation, caught Shotgun Sallie behind the knees, and knocked her to the floor. On the way down her finger jerked against the second trigger and the shotgun boomed in the small confines of Longarm's apartment, disintegrating Longarm's bedside table, water pitcher, and glass.

Longarm rolled out of the bed and managed to reach the enraged woman before she could unholster the gun belted on her shapely hip. Even at that he would have failed if Doc Potter hadn't also grabbed Shotgun Sallie around the legs and helped keep her down.

"I'm going to kill you, Custis Long!" Shotgun Sallie swore.

"Then I'm afraid that you'll have to get in line behind at least four others," he replied. "Shotgun, quit struggling and display some good sense."

"Screw you!"

"I'm not up to that tonight," he said, grinning foolishly. "But in your case I might try to make a heroic exception."

A long string of cuss words erupted from Shotgun Sallie's lips but Longarm didn't mind. He liked to see fire in a beautiful woman, so long as she wasn't trying to blow him all to hell.

Chapter 6

"Would you just simmer down and stop fighting us!" Long-arm yelled into Shotgun Sallie's face. "We're all trying to do the same thing."

"And what would that be?" she demanded.

"We all want to find out who ambushed your sister and me out on the South Platte River."

Shotgun Sallie, having no choice, finally stopped struggling. "Let me up," she grated.

"Only if you promise not to try to kill us."

"I'm not big on keeping my promises, Marshal."

"Listen to me," Dr. Potter said to the woman. "You just saved both of our lives, and right now there's a dead man downstairs in the alley and he might be someone we recognize so that we can stop the others from trying to carry out this vendetta."

"You won't be able to recognize him," Shotgun Sallie said, "because I plumb blew the sonofabitch's head off his shoulders."

"But he might be carrying some identification," Doc

Potter insisted. "The point is that you and I need to go down and take a look at the body."

Shotgun Sallie glared at Longarm. "What about you, Marshal?"

"I don't think I'm up for that right this moment," he told her. "But Doc Potter is right. You did save our lives and now you need to go down and try to identify the body even if the head is blown off. Because if we can figure out who the man is, then we can find the others who are responsible for killing your sister, Lucy."

"I hold *you* responsible, Lawman!"

"And I don't blame you a bit for feeling that way," Longarm told the angry woman in the hope of calming her down. "But we can sort that business out after we find the *other* killers."

"What's this '*we*' bullshit?" Shotgun Sallie demanded.

Longarm shrugged. "Since we're both looking for the same people, I just thought that . . ."

"You're a federal marshal! You'd want to arrest those bastards while I mean to blow them all to hell! So, Marshal, I damn sure don't think that we'd make a very good team."

"I can understand why you'd think that way," Longarm said, "but the truth of the matter is that I've given up my badge. Or at least, I intend to give it up as soon as I can walk into the Federal Building and tell my boss, Marshal Billy Vail, that I'm resigning."

"Do you really mean that?" Shotgun Sallie asked, studying his face closely.

"I sure do." Longarm's voice hardened. "I want revenge for Lucy's death every bit as much as you do."

"That's not possible. But let me up and I promise I'll not try to kill either of you."

"Glad you're a reasonable thinking woman," Doc Potter said, releasing her.

Shotgun Sallie climbed to her feet and smoothed her shirt. She reloaded her shotgun, and that gave Longarm an uneasy moment until she said, "All right, Doc. Let's you and me find a lantern and go see what's left of that jasper I just ventilated."

"Sounds like a fine idea," Doc said, shooting Longarm a nervous glance. "Custis, get back in that bed. I'll do a postmortem examination and come right back up here to tell you what I have found or couldn't find out about the man who tried to kill us a few minutes ago."

"Be careful, Doc. That one probably has at least four friends hanging around Denver."

"Don't think that hasn't already occurred to me," Potter said as he headed out the doorway.

"Don't you go anywhere while I'm down there," Shotgun Sallie warned, giving Longarm a backward glance at the doorway. "Because you can't run away from me. I'll find you no matter what hole you choose for hiding."

"I've never hidden from anyone, Shotgun, and I won't start now because I'll be right here," Longarm said, raising his Colt to show that he was now armed and prepared to defend himself. "But you had better announce yourself loud and clear when you come back up those stairs and knock on my door."

"I will," she promised. "Because you and me have things to sort out concerning my dead sister."

"I expect we do," Longarm answered as Shotgun Sallie disappeared following the doctor.

About a half hour later, Shotgun Sallie and Dr. Potter came trooping up the stairs and when they knocked, Longarm bid them entry with a gun in his hand. The pair stood side by side at the foot of his bed, and even the doctor, who had seen a lot of death, appeared shaken by the headless body he'd just examined down in the alley.

"I'm going to help myself to that bottle of whiskey you spoke about earlier," Doc said, not waiting for an invitation.

"Help yourself, Doc. You too, Shotgun."

"Believe I will," she said, trying to keep her voice steady.

"And I wouldn't mind a glass myself," Longarm called. "Make it a full one.

When all three of them had whiskey, Longarm sat up in his bed and said, "Doc, what did you find out from examining the body?"

"I found out exactly what a powerful shotgun blast to the back of a human head will do to that same human's face." There was a long pause, then, "Namely, blow it apart. Custis, there was nothing left of the face except fragments of bone, blood, and brain."

The doctor drained his glass of whiskey and took a refill; Longarm saw that the man's normally steady hand now had a pronounced tremor. "Custis, I've never seen such physical trauma in my life."

"Was there anything on his body that would help us figure out who he was or where he came from?"

"Nothing," the doctor said, quickly taking another gulp. "From the body's skin, my professional opinion is that the deceased was probably in his late twenties, although he could have been a few years older."

"Black hair? Brown hair?"

"Black . . . I think."

"Well dressed?"

Doctor Potter shook his head. "No. He was very poorly

dressed. His boots were run down at the heels and his shirt was frayed at the sleeves and collar. He was dirty and his fingernails were crusted underneath with mud and grime."

"Anything else?" Longarm asked with mounting exasperation.

"Not that I could see. The light down in that alley is poor despite all the lanterns that are on the death scene. While I was trying to do some kind of examination, Marshal Duncan was shouting and having his usual fit. I swear that man is going to die soon of heart failure."

"That would be a blessing to the town," Longarm said dryly. Then he looked at Shotgun Sallie. "Was there anything that you saw that might help us identify the man?"

"He was big-boned and his hands were thick with calluses. I'd say that he was a miner or a prospector rather than a cowboy or ordinary working man. And he had a type of fancy belt buckle that I've seen before up in the mining district."

Longarm's interest sharpened. "Which 'district' would that be?"

"Up around Granite Creek."

"And exactly how would you know a thing like that?" Dr. Potter asked, frowning.

"Because I owned a whorehouse up there up until five years ago when I sold it to my favorite working girls and bought another whorehouse up in Central City."

"You're a *madam*?" Longarm asked with surprise.

Shotgun Sallie nodded. "That's right. I started out like most do. But unlike most I saved my money and worked my way off of the bed and into my own business. A small hotel in Cripple Creek, then a bigger hotel and saloon with a whorehouse upstairs. I sold it for a tidy profit and moved up to Central City and bought the biggest whorehouse in town . . . as well as a cattle ranch that loses almost as much money each year as my whorehouse earns."

"How'd you come by your name?" the doctor asked.

"I killed a couple of bastards in my Cripple Creek whorehouse with a shotgun. You want to know the particulars, Doc?"

He shook his head and took another deep gulp of whiskey. "I don't believe I do, Shotgun."

"Then don't ask me any more personal questions."

Longarm could tell that Dr. Potter was shaken by the body but also shocked by Shotgun Sallie's candid admission concerning her past and present circumstances. But as for himself, Longarm thought that the woman showed an unusual amount of intelligence and grit. Every whore he'd ever arrested or known had always held on to the same dream: being able to save up enough money to become a madam or get out of the business entirely before age, disease, or violence put an end to their sordid lives. Shotgun Sallie appeared to be one of the very few who had actually managed to escape from prostitution. And looking at her now, he supposed that was in good part due to the fact that she was extremely good-looking and shapely, which meant that she would have commanded top dollar for her early sexual favors.

"Have you seen any of those belt buckles anywhere else?" Longarm asked the woman.

"Nope. They're round with a silver dollar in the middle, and the silver dollar is encircled by some fancy etching . . . the kind that a very good silversmith would do on a pair of spurs, for example."

Longarm thought about that for a moment and then turned his attention to the doctor. "How soon can I travel?"

"By horse or by buggy?"

"Whatever I can do the soonest."

"You're feverish and you've lost a lot of blood," Dr. Potter said. "I wouldn't advise you leaving that bed for at least a couple of weeks."

"That's not reasonable, Doc."

"From a medical point of view, it's entirely reasonable."

Longarm and the doctor did a long stare-down and finally it was the doctor who looked away as he finished his second glass of whiskey and then slowly reached for his hat. "I should go home now because my wife is waiting and will be very worried. I imagine that Marshal Duncan will want me to file some report since I was here when the shooting occurred."

"I'm not filing any damned report," Shotgun Sallie pronounced. "I'll talk to your town lawman, but I'm not going to sit in front of the man and answer a bunch of damned fool questions."

"Marshal Duncan can be overbearing, to put it lightly," Longarm informed the woman.

"Then *you* handle your Marshal Duncan," Shotgun Sallie told him, "because I'm going to get some sleep and tomorrow I'm going to start hunting the rest of that bunch. How many more are there?"

Longarm scowled. "There were five hooded riders when your sister and I were attacked at the river while having a picnic. Before going on that picnic, I was jumped by a man at Drury Stables and I shot him dead. So there might have been six men that started out if that man was party to the others."

"If you killed one of them at the stables and I just blew one's head off his damned shoulders, then that means there are at least four left that need immediate killing." Shotgun's eyes tightened at the corners. "Does the math make sense to you, Lawman?"

"Yes, it does," Longarm said. "But I want you to wait until I can help you find and kill them."

"I don't give a tinker's damn what you want or don't want, Lawman. And I'm sure not waiting around while you recuperate." She started to leave and then stopped. "By the way, Lawman, what color horses were those five riding when they jumped you and my sister along the river?"

Longarm almost told Shotgun Sallie that three were dark-colored horses, but the other two were a pinto and a bald-faced buckskin. Instead, he checked his response and said, "I have no idea."

"No idea?" the woman said, cradling her shotgun in her arms. "How the hell could that be?"

"It all happened very, very fast," Longarm replied.

"Did you even *try* to defend my sister's life?" Shotgun Sallie demanded, her voice heavy with scorn.

"I was unarmed," he said, knowing that it sounded weak. "Lucy and I were cooling off in the river and my gun and rifle were out of reach. The only thing we could do was try to get into the deepest part of the river and escape with our lives."

Shotgun Sallie shook her head. "What kind of a federal marshal are you, anyway? You take my sister out there and you weren't even man enough to defend her?"

"I'm sorry."

"You are sorry indeed," Shotgun Sallie pronounced. "And if that were not so I would shoot you this minute. But, as it is, I guess I'll just go and start hunting for those other men."

"I still wish you'd wait for me to help."

Shotgun Sallie started to say something, but then seemed to change her mind and left without another word.

"Custis?"

Longarm looked at his friend. "Yeah, Doc?"

"You'd be wise to stay well clear of Shotgun Sallie. That woman is on a mission and she's as likely to kill you, me, or anyone else as she is her sister's real murderers."

"I know that."

"Then just stay in bed for a while and let her go about her bloody revenge."

"Can't do that, Doc."

"Why the hell not!" the doctor said, his voice a little slurred and filled with exasperation.

"Because Shotgun Sallie and I want exactly the same thing, and that's the blood of whoever killed Miss Lucy Coyle and almost killed me."

"Are you really going to give up your federal officer's badge?"

"I am," Longarm told the man. "First thing tomorrow morning."

"You're not strong enough to go to the Federal Building and walk up all those stone steps."

"Don't bet on that, Doc."

The doctor shook his head and then left Longarm alone with his dark and deadly thoughts of revenge.

Chapter 7

Longarm woke up the next morning feeling as if he might live after all. His fever was gone and he was very weak but determined to get out of his apartment and go see his boss, Billy Vail. There, he would hand over his badge and thus free himself from any restraints imposed by his job as a federal marshal.

Getting dressed was slow going, but he managed. When he was ready to leave, he buckled on his Colt revolver, butt forward on his left hip, placed his hideout derringer in his vest pocket attached to his watch fob, and put on his flat-brimmed and snuff brown hat.

Longarm studied his scratched and battered face in the mirror, noting his sunken cheeks and the dark hollows under his eyes. He looked like walking death, but no matter. He'd lain around long enough, and it was time to seek revenge for the murder of Miss Lucy Coyle.

The U.S. Marshal's office was located near the Denver Mint on Colfax Avenue. As he slowly walked up the street he noted the crest of Capitol Hill, which was crowned by the gold dome of the Colorado State Capitol Building. It was a fine morning but he found he tired quickly, and he was glad when he arrived at the Federal Building and slowly climbed the many stone stairs. Keeping his hat low over his brow, Longarm tried to avoid conversation or attracting anyone's attention. Everyone in this building would know about the man he'd shot at the Drury Stables and also about the death of Lucy Coyle while out on a picnic with him just days before. The subject was painful and personal and Longarm simply did not wish to discuss the matter with anyone other than his boss and dear friend.

"Custis!" Billy Vail exclaimed, jumping up from behind his large oak desk. "I was just about to tell my secretary that I was heading over to your apartment to see how you were feeling."

"As you can see," Longarm replied, "not too well."

"You look awful! Should you even be up and around?"

"Dr. Potter thinks not, but you know I'm not a good patient."

"Sit down," Billy urged. "You look so weak I expect you might fall over at any minute."

"I'm strong enough to have walked all the way from my place to here," Longarm informed his boss as he took a chair. "But I have to admit that walking was probably foolish."

"I heard about the shooting at Drury Stables on Sunday morning," Billy said. "And then about the terrible murder of Miss Coyle later that same day. I understand that you were ambushed."

"That's right," Longarm said. "But Lucy took a bullet instead of me and now she's dead."

"I'm very sorry, Custis. I never had the pleasure of meeting the young woman, but I've heard that she was a real peach and very highly thought of in the community."

"She was," Longarm replied. "I was . . . was quite taken with Miss Coyle and her death has hit me hard. I feel responsible for her loss and I mean to bring all the killers to justice."

"Any idea who attacked you?"

"None whatsoever. But I think that the man I killed at Drury Stables was connected to the five hooded horsemen who set upon me and Miss Lucy out on the South Platte River."

Billy pursed his lips and leaned back in his office chair. "So you believe there were initially *six* men gunning for you?"

"That's right. And last night, another attempt was made to kill me at my apartment."

Billy's jaw dropped in amazement. "No!"

"Yes. Doc Potter was there and we were almost murdered. I had a gun hidden under my bedsheet and might have been able to shoot the man, but Miss Lucy's sister, Shotgun Sallie, saved me the trouble."

Billy shook his head as if to clear it and then asked, "Are you saying a woman named Shotgun Sallie killed another one of the gang that has been trying to kill you?"

"Yep. Her shotgun blast knocked the man right through my window and he fell into the alley. But he was dead long before he hit the ground. Blew his head plumb off."

"This is . . . well, incredible!"

"Sure made a mess in my apartment."

"Who—?"

"We don't know who the man was because his face was blown away," Longarm interrupted. "I'm sad to say that there was just no way to identify the body."

Billy reached into his humidor for a pair of cigars, lit a match and held it out to Longarm. "I'm completely aghast at what you've just told me, Custis. But what immediately comes to mind is, who would be so bold as to come after you? And why?"

"Those are the questions," Longarm replied, inhaling the tobacco and then exhaling it toward the ceiling.

"And who is this wild, deadly woman with the remarkable name who blew the man's head off in your apartment?"

"She's a madam who owns a prosperous whorehouse up in Central City. Her business must be doing pretty well because she also owns a cattle ranch not far away."

"But what connection does she have to . . .?"

"As I mentioned, she is Miss Lucy Coyle's sister. Lucy never even told me she had a sister, for reasons that have now become obvious. Lucy was a churchgoing woman and the last thing she would have wanted to tell me was that her sister owned and operated a thriving whorehouse."

Billy nodded. "Yes, I can certainly understand that. What is this Central City woman like?"

"She's the exact opposite of Lucy. Profane. Hard as nails."

"You'd have to be hard to be successful in her business. She probably started off as a working girl."

"I'm not entirely sure that's the case," Longarm said. "But I have to tell you that Shotgun Sallie is even better looking than her younger sister . . . in a way."

"What way?"

Longarm studied the tip of his cigar. "Shotgun Sallie has animal magnetism. When a man looks at Shotgun Sallie, the first thing he wants to do is jump her . . . but then he looks again and he thinks that could be a fatal mistake. Even so, there's something about her that you just can't push out of your mind."

"Custis!" Billy exclaimed. "The woman blew a man's

head off in your apartment and you're actually telling me that you find her . . . attractive?"

"Yep, and I know that sounds crazy because she hates my guts. Blames me for the death of her sister . . . which I fully understand. And you know what else?"

"No," Billy replied. "You've hit me with such shocking news that I simply have no idea what you could have left out."

"Shotgun Sallie has sworn to find and kill the remaining four men that ambushed and shot her sister."

"Are you saying that she's going to hunt them down right here in Denver with a big shotgun?"

"That's *exactly* what she has in mind."

"But the newspaper this morning says that the killers were all hooded. And you admitted that you couldn't identify the one whose head she blew apart."

"And so," Longarm concluded, "your next question is . . . how can Shotgun possibly find out who the last four murderers are?"

"That was my question."

"And my answer is that I have no earthly idea how she intends to find them. But I do know this. From what I've seen of the woman, she won't rest until she has avenged the death of her sister, Lucy Coyle. And here's the last thing I wanted you to know, Boss. I'm resigning my office and I'm also going to find the murderers and take revenge if it's the last thing on earth that I ever do."

To make his point, Longarm reached into his vest pocket, took out his badge, and placed it on Billy Vail's desk.

"You can't be serious!"

"It's something I just have to do," Longarm explained. "It's driving me almost insane living with the knowledge that Lucy would be alive if I hadn't taken her on that picnic. I'll never have any peace until I bring those men to justice."

"Yes, *justice*! That's the important word here, Custis. And justice means the law. Arrest, a trial by a jury of the accused's peers, and then a lawful sentencing. I have no doubt that the sentence would be death, but it has to be a sentence, not an *execution by your hands*."

Longarm smoked in silence for a moment, trying to phrase the words that would make his point more convincing to a man who had devoted his life to upholding the law of the land. "Billy, do you know how many years I have worked for you?"

"Seven or eight. Maybe more, but . . ."

"And I've always upheld the law. Isn't that right?"

"You *bend* the law to get the job done," Billy corrected. "And we both know full well that there have been many, many times that you've come just a hairsbreadth away from committing a breach of your oath of office."

"That's true enough, I suppose," Longarm admitted. "But this time I'm going to step over the line because I'm convinced that the surviving members of this gang won't rest until I'm dead."

"But . . ."

"Hear me out," Longarm insisted. "You weren't out on the South Platte River on Sunday, so you have no idea how determined those horsemen were to kill me. If a cat has nine lives, then I must have used double that number just on Sunday. Those men are as bent on killing me as Shotgun Sallie and I are on killing them. And so this is something that will end in the grave."

"But, Custis, a hangman's noose is the justified end."

"That's not going to happen," Longarm predicted. "And I can't tell you why, but I just know it down deep in the marrow of my bones. These men won't quit until I'm dead and I won't quit until they are all dead. It's really pretty simple."

"And unlawful."

"Yeah," Longarm agreed. "It is, and that's why I'm leaving my badge on your desk and walking out of here a simple civilian, because if I kept my badge, the fallout would come down on your head as well as mine. And we've been friends too long for me to allow that kind of trouble to come your way. If I gunned down the last four gang members as a badge-toting federal marshal, it would probably cost you your job. I'm carrying around more than enough guilt right now and I won't take any more. You have a lovely wife and children to support and I'm not going to put their livelihoods in jeopardy."

Billy smoked quietly for a moment, and then asked, "And that's your final decision?"

"Afraid so."

"Anything I can do to help you?"

"There is," Longarm said. "You've got the files from all the arrests and cases I've been involved in since working for you. Have a file clerk or someone go through all those files and try to dig up someone that would want me dead at any cost."

"In your distinguished but bloody career you haven't left a lot of survivors," Billy said. "The men you've brought to justice are all either dead . . . or rotting in prison."

"Some have been released and a few have probably escaped prison. Also, it's possible that someone I've killed or sent to prison had sons or other relatives that are now out to get me."

"I don't think that we'll find anyone whose death or imprisonment would cause six men to want you dead."

"I don't expect you to find them either," Longarm said. "But at this point, I've almost nothing to go on."

"What do you mean, 'almost'," Billy asked.

"In the split second I had before diving into the river I saw that two of the five mounted horsemen were riding off-colored horses . . . one a pinto and the other a buckskin."

"There are a lot of those in Denver. Probably a hundred or more."

"Maybe not to be found as a pair," Longarm said. "And Shotgun Sallie says she thinks that the man who tried to kill me in my apartment is a miner or prospector from up around Granite Creek because of his unusual silver dollar belt buckle and all the heavy calluses on his hands."

"That's terribly thin," Billy mused.

"I know that, but it's a start. Right now, Shotgun Sallie is probably prowling Denver looking for a matching belt buckle even knowing what a weak link that might be to the killers."

"Custis, that woman sounds like she ought to be put in jail or a mental institution. Surely you must realize that a shotgun fired haphazardly on a crowded city street can be a deadly disaster."

"I don't think Shotgun Sallie is 'haphazard' about anything she does."

"You hope she's not. If she opens up with a big shotgun and wipes out innocent pedestrians, that isn't going to sit too well on your already overburdened conscience."

"I'll try to locate her and then reason with her," Longarm offered. "But, frankly, since she despises and blames me for the death of her sister, I believe that anything I try to say to the woman might actually be counterproductive."

"A lovely, deadly loose cannon?"

"That is an accurate description of Shotgun Sallie," Longarm said, nodding his head.

Billy reached out and picked up the badge that Longarm had just offered. "How about I just hold the paperwork on your resignation until we have some time to work on this?"

"Billy, if you do that and I'm in the middle of a blood-bath, you won't be able to say that I resigned. So put in the paperwork and make my resignation official *today*."

"If you absolutely insist."

"I do absolutely insist."

"All right," Billy said with unconcealed reluctance. "But I'm going to tell you something important and that is that I'm going to join the hunt for the men that tried to kill you and did kill Miss Lucy Coyle."

"If you become involved the field is gonna get sorta crowded."

"In this case," Billy said, "the more the better."

"Maybe. Maybe not," Longarm told his boss as he climbed to his feet.

"This is going to end soon," Billy said. "And whatever happens, Custis, I want you to know that I will do everything within my legal means to help you."

"A man couldn't possibly ask for more," Longarm said, shaking Billy's hand and then heading out of his office door.

Chapter 8

Shotgun Sallie did not want to attract anyone's attention. By now, the front pages of every Denver newspaper contained the gory and lurid accounts of "the man with no head" who had been found in the alley directly below Longarm's upstairs apartment. There had been no quotes or interviews in the newspaper with Custis Long, but reporters had questioned Dr. Potter in great detail, and so it was known that a woman had been the shooter. Headlines proclaimed her a "Murder Mystery Woman" and the "Deadly Damsel" among other ridiculous things and there was an intense citywide curiosity regarding her real name and identity, which the doctor had thankfully refused to reveal.

Shotgun Sallie knew that she was supposed to stop by the local marshal's office to make a report, but she figured the hell with that obligation. Newspaper reporters were swarming around Marshal Oscar Duncan's office like flies around fresh shit, and the very last thing that she wanted to do was answer a bunch of fool questions. She supposed that they would eventually discover that she was a madam up in Central City, a bit of information that would cause even more sensationalism. Sure, it might help her brothel business, but Shotgun Sallie didn't think that it was worth the bother. And far more important, she did not want everyone in Denver to know that she had been Lucy Coyle's soiled sister . . . a former whore and now a successful madam.

So, as the day passed, Shotgun Sallie, dressed in a long overcoat and wearing a slouched hat with her hair tucked up under it, stalked Denver looking for the last four men who had murdered her sister. She didn't stop anyone or ask anyone questions, but she watched and walked the streets with her shotgun tucked under her long overcoat, her eyes missing nothing.

The trouble was that she had no idea who the four remaining killers were or what they looked like. Given that great handicap, the best she could hope for was to see four hard-looking and well-armed men moving together, and that one of them was wearing a fancy silver dollar belt buckle similar to the one she'd seen the day before.

"Mister, can you spare a man the cost of a meal and drink?" a pathetic-looking man in rags asked, stepping directly into Shotgun Sallie's path. "I'm awful hungry and thirsty. Been havin' a real bad run of luck lately. Sure could use a little change out of your pocket to buy me a cheap meal."

In her high-heeled boots, Shotgun Sallie was almost as tall as the ragged man. She looked into his unshaven face and saw eyes that reflected hopelessness and misery. She could smell his rank odor and doubted if he had had a bath for weeks, perhaps even months.

"How old are you?" she asked.

"I'm forty-two, mister."

"What do you do for a living?"

He shrugged, not meeting her eyes. "Mostly nothin' at all these hard days."

"I think that you mostly beg for money and drinks," Shotgun Sallie told him. "And from the look and smell of you, if you don't get sober and start taking care of yourself, you'll probably be dead before next winter."

The ragged beggar bristled and straightened just a little, pulling his chin up and pushing his narrow shoulders back. "Mister, I asked you for a few coins, not a sermon. Are you a preacher or something, trying to sell me religion?"

"Naw. That's the last thing I'd try to be. But I'm hungry," she said, ignoring his question. "And just a few doors up is a café. How about you and me go into it and order a big steak, potatoes, and maybe some apple pie and coffee?"

The beggar stared at her through his red and rheumy eyes. "You offering to buy me a steak?"

"That's right."

"Why?"

"Because I'm not in the mood to eat alone and you look hungry."

"Oh, I am that," he said. "Thirsty, too. Real thirsty, in fact." His eyes narrowed. "That's why I'd far rather you bought me a few drinks at a saloon where they have pickled eggs and maybe some fried pork rinds or some such thing to chew on."

"I know, but that's not my offer. I'm asking if you would like to have a steak, potatoes, coffee, and some apple pie. All you have to do is tell me yes or no."

"If I say no, you ain't going to give me even the price of a damned beer, are you?" he said truculently.

"Nope."

The beggar sighed, and then looked across the street at a saloon with sad, longing eyes. "All right," he said finally. "I'll eat a steak with you."

"Hope you don't think you're doing me any favors," Shotgun Sallie said with a wry smile.

"I ain't thinkin' that way, only I wish instead of the coffee and pie, you'd at least buy me a glass of beer or two to help with the steak." He held up his dirty hands and they were shaking badly. "As you can see, I'm not even sure I can hold a fork or a knife because of my shakes."

Shotgun Sallie felt a momentary surge of pity. This man was truly in desperate shape. "Maybe a beer," she hedged.

The beggar grinned, showing a lot of missing teeth. "Mister, I sure am grateful to you!"

"What's your name?" she asked.

"Bertram Hollister. And yours, if I may be so bold?"

"Just call me . . . Samaritan."

The drunk looked confused. "Why that's an almighty strange name. Never heard anyone named that before. Does everyone call you Sam for short like they call me Bert?"

"No, but you can call me Sam if you want. Now, Bert, let's get us some food. I'm so hungry I could eat a sow and her nine piglets and then chase her boar a mile with a sharp knife and fork."

Bert laughed a dry, cackling laugh, but it was surprisingly strong and good to hear.

As they headed for the café, Shotgun Sallie wondered if she was making a mistake helping out this poor wreckage of a human being. She didn't want Bertram Hollister to realize her notoriety but, from the looks of him, he probably hadn't read a newspaper or even heard about the man whose head she'd blown apart the night before. However,

Bertram Hollister easily might just have seen some tough strangers prowling the streets or saloons. And maybe he'd even been in a saloon and overheard something that would help her find the killers. Probably not, but at least she would be doing a simple act of kindness for this lost soul.

"Can I have that beer first?" he asked.

"I guess you can."

"Probably one before we eat and one to wash down the steak is what I really need."

"I understand, Bert."

"I'm glad that you do. I'll wash up in that horse trough out in front of the café before I go in."

"That's a good idea," she said. "Dunk your face in the water and wipe it clean."

"I'll do 'er, Sam."

The steak had been juicy and rare, the potatoes fried in tasty grease, the coffee strong, and the apple pie delicious. Bert had inhaled two glasses of beer before the food had arrived and then begged for more, but she'd refused and he'd dug into his steak like a starving wolf. His hands had become steady enough to hold a fork to his mouth and to cut his meat. Now, with coffee and solid food in his belly, Bert looked as if he were about to fall asleep at the table.

"Bert," she said, "don't doze off on me yet. I have a few questions to ask you."

He roused himself. "Shoot, Sam."

Shotgun Sallie had kept her overcoat on in the café, her hat pulled low and her sawed-off, double-barreled shotgun tight at her side to avoid anyone's attention. The shotgun had kept slipping and she'd finally just placed it against the wall between herself and the rest of the room. So far, no one had paid her or the deadly shotgun the least bit of attention.

"Bert, I'm looking for four men."

He actually grinned. "Any particular four?"

"Yes. Did you hear about that woman who was murdered in the South Platte River last Sunday?"

"I'd have to be deaf as a post not have heard about her. Poor woman. People are saying that she was swimmin' naked in the river with some marshal when they were both set upon." Bert leaned forward and whispered, "I'll bet she was eatin' something longer than a pickle at the picnic that afternoon."

Bert giggled and it was all that Shotgun Sallie could do not to put her steak knife in his throat. She collected herself and managed to ask, "Have you seen any strangers that look real hard around Denver town? One of them wearing a silver dollar in his belt buckle?"

"Why you askin' me that?"

Shotgun Sallie suddenly had a revelation and knew what to say in response. "Bert, there's a bounty on those woman killers. A big bounty, and if you could help me find them, I'd be willing to split the bounty with you."

"How much of a bounty?"

"A hundred dollars for each killer," she lied. "That would be at least four or five hundred dollars."

Bert's eyes lit up and he leaned forward. "And I'd get half?"

"Yes."

He swallowed hard. "But, Sam, would I have to . . . ?"

"No, no," she said quickly. "All you'd have to do is to help me find them and I'd do the rest."

Bert looked closely at her. "You wouldn't try to . . . arrest 'em all by yourself, would you?"

"No, of course not," she assured him. "Do I look dumb?"

"Well, you bought me . . . a dirty drunk . . . a steak, didn't you?"

"Yes, but I thought you might just be the kind of man who gets around town and sees things. Sees everything, in fact."

"I see a lot," he confided. "Most of it ugly. Denver has a lot of big buildings, people dressed up real fine and ladies as pretty as princesses, but it's a tough and mean town, Sam, and real hard on drunks. Why, that Marshal Duncan and his deputies . . . they don't put me in jail and feed me anymore. No, sir. They haul me into an alley and beat the hell outa me! They always tell me to get out of town or to hurry up and die."

Bertram Hollister's eyes filled with bitter tears that leaked down his dirty cheeks. "Last time I passed out on the sidewalk they put the boots to me real hard. Doc Potter, he can tell you that the marshal and his deputies hate me hangin' around. Doc is the only good man I've met in Denver. All the rest . . . 'cept you, Sam . . . are stingy and self-righteous sonsabitches."

"If you help me find those killers, you'd have enough money to take a stagecoach out of Denver and go to almost anyplace you'd like," she told him. "Is there anyplace else you really want to be, Bert?"

"Maybe I'd go back to Durango," he sniffled. "Got a daughter there and I lived with her and her husband for a while. Then I got to drinkin' so fierce they didn't want me around the family anymore. I don't blame them one damn bit. Sure miss 'em at times, though."

"Bert, what did you do before you . . ." She didn't quite know how to phrase her question without hurting his already whiskey-shattered feelings.

"Got old and drunk?" Bert asked.

"Yeah," Shotgun Sallie said. "What did you do when you were a young and healthy man?"

"I was a first-rate cowboy," he said with obvious pride. "I drove cattle on the long drives up from Texas, I did. And I was a top hand. I could ride out them broncs, too. Ride 'em as good as any man and I broke 'em to be fine ranch horses. Never was cruel to no horse I broke. But some of 'em . . . well, there were some that threw me farther than a Death Valley buzzard could smell a dry canteen. There were times that I was bucked so high in the air that I could say all my prayers before I hit the ground."

"Bert, I've got a ranch up near Central City. I run about three hundred head of cattle and raise maybe sixty horses."

"Sixty?"

"Yeah. I like horses," Shotgun Sallie confessed. "I don't make a lot of money on 'em, but I don't lose any, either."

"You got some good cowboys and bronc busters on your payroll?" he asked.

"I've got a few, but I could always use another."

Their eyes met but then Bert quickly looked away. "I ain't never going to be able to ride broncs again, Sam. I'm too old, broken, and worn out. Too drunk and too tired."

"I could use a good and reliable stableman," she said without hesitation. "Someone to look out for the horses. Feed in the winter. Help me at foaling time. Doctor a horse when it's sick. Muck stalls. Pitch hay and straw. Repair saddles and bridles."

"I could do all that. I ain't a-kiddin' you, Sam, I really do know an awful lot about horses."

"I'll just bet you do." She placed her hand on his thin shoulder. "My place is about three miles west of Central

City. Ranch is called Shotgun. You wouldn't have any trouble finding it."

"'Shotgun' is the name of your ranch?"

"That's right. It's the Shotgun Ranch."

"You sure do go in for strange names," Bert said. "Samaritan. Shotgun Ranch."

"Remember that name and maybe someday stop on by even if you and I don't find those killers and get the reward. But I won't let you on the property if you're drunk. You'd have to be sober to work for me, Bert."

"I . . . I might be able to do that," he said. "I ain't completely given up on myself yet. And I still like horses a lot more than people."

"Think hard about my offer," she said. "I'll probably be back here same time tomorrow, hungry as I was today. If you see me, come join me for another steak."

"I . . . I just don't know what to say about you and your generosity, Sam."

"You don't have to say anything," she told him. "But if you see four hard men with one of them wearing a silver dollar on his belt buckle, you be sure and come to tell me real fast."

"Where can I find you?"

She hadn't even gotten a hotel room. "Where's a good, clean hotel here in Denver?"

"If you can afford it, try the Heritage House," he said. "It's almost directly across the street."

"I'll do it. That's where you can find me if I'm not out looking for those killers."

Bert nodded. "Don't suppose you got a little change in your pocket for a whiskey?"

"Sorry, Bert. I want you looking for those four men, not

getting the shit kicked out of you in an alley by the town marshal or his damned deputies."

"Understood," he said, managing a smile before he walked away with a backhand wave of his dirt-crusted fingers.

Chapter 9

The next day, Shotgun Sallie was out prowling the streets of Denver again, and when afternoon rolled around and she had not seen anyone that even remotely aroused her suspicion, she started looking for Bertram Hollister, thinking that he might be hungry and need another good meal. Sure, the man was a drunk and a pathetic derelict, but long ago she'd found that she had a soft place in her heart for lost souls. Old or diseased whores were at the top of the sympathy list of people that could break her heart and that she would always help; drunks and crippled-up cowboys fit into the same category.

Shotgun Sallie recalled Bertram Hollister remarking over his steak that he slept in a livery barn just a few blocks away and that in repayment he helped clean stalls when he was feeling up to the chore. The livery he slept in at night was called the Salty's Stables.

"Excuse me?" she said, stepping into Salty's old and badly listing wooden barn. "Anyone here?"

No one answered.

"Bert? Bert, are you in here? I'm getting hungry and

thought you might want another steak and that maybe you'd seen someone that fit the description I gave you of those killers."

In reply, a horse whinnied nervously from somewhere in the gloom. Shotgun Sallie walked deeper into the barn that seemed to be empty of life except for that one horse in the back stomping and whinnying.

"Bertram Hollister? It's me, Samaritan."

She heard a soft groan and stepped forward, drawing her shotgun out from under her overcoat. "Bert?"

Another groan and then she was rushing forward to nearly stumble over the drunken old cowboy.

"Bert! What's wrong?"

"Hurt bad." He was fighting for every breath. "Think I'm gonna die this time."

She laid her shotgun down in the darkness and knelt beside Bertram Hollister. "What happened?"

"A deputy found me drinkin' and I guess . . ." Bert coughed and wheezed. "Guess he didn't have anything better to do for fun than draggin' me into an alley and beatin' me last night."

"*Which* deputy?"

"Name is Clausen. Bobbie Clausen. Mean little bastard. He's hit and kicked me around some before, but not this bad. This time . . . this time he might have finished the job."

"I'm going to get you a doctor," Shotgun Sallie told the man. "I'll be right back!"

"Save your money for . . . for your nice horses."

Shotgun Sallie knew where Dr. Potter's office was and she ran out of the barn not even aware that her long brown hair had fallen out from under her hat. She was racing up the street when a man in the shadows of a building stepped out and took dead aim on her with a revolver.

Unarmed, Shotgun Sallie dove behind a wagon as two bullets whip-cracked inches past her head. She looked up and saw the face of the man that was trying to kill her, and it was an ugly and hate-filled one. The man was about twenty-five, big and tall with wild red hair. People on the street were shouting in alarm and scattering in all directions as Sallie huddled behind the wagon, its driver holding his hands up to the sky and yelling at the top of his lungs.

The red-haired man wanted to come at her close so that he could not miss a third time. Shotgun Sallie could see it in his eyes, but now there were too many witnesses, too many Denver men packing their own guns, men who might decide that a midday execution of a young woman with long brown hair was unacceptable. The redheaded man screamed at her from fifty paces, "You killed my brother. Shot his head off, and by gawd you are a walking dead woman!"

Shotgun Sallie's hands clenched and unclenched. If she had her shotgun now she would have charged the gunman and one of them would have been dead in the next minute. But since she was unarmed there was nothing to do but crouch behind cover and wait for this to play out.

"A *dead* woman!" he screamed again.

"I see your face, you ugly sonofabitch!" Shotgun Sallie yelled. "I'll find and kill you and the other cowards!"

The man cursed and disappeared at a hard run. Shotgun Sallie had a moment of indecision and then she realized that it would be crazy to go after the red-haired man without a weapon. So she jumped up from behind the wagon and continued on to get the doctor.

"Bert is going to live, but he's got at least four or five broken ribs," Dr. Potter announced. "He's going to need some attention, and given his sad physical condition, even then he may catch pneumonia or just die of those chest and facial injuries."

"Bert told me that Deputy Bob Clausen did that to him last night."

"Clausen is meaner than a teased rattlesnake," the doctor said. "If Bert is willing to swear out a complaint, perhaps we can get a judge to . . ."

"He won't do that," Sallie snapped. "I know that much about Bert. He'd be afraid of getting an even worse beating if he lodged a formal complaint. Besides, he's a town drunk. Don't you think that the deputy would just claim that he was trying to arrest Bert when the man got rowdy and started fighting him? Or that he found Bert in that condition and maybe brought him back to that stable? Whose word would a judge take? The word of a sworn officer of the law . . . or that of Bert Hollister the drunk?"

"Yeah," Doc said, "I see your point and you're right. But Bert was severely beaten and Deputy Clausen should never be allowed to get away with something that hateful and vicious."

"He *won't* get away with it," Shotgun Sallie vowed. "I'll make sure of that."

"Now wait a minute, Miss. I was there when you blew that man's head off up in Longarm's apartment with your shotgun. And the only reason you aren't cooling your heels in Marshal Oscar Duncan's jail and facing prison is because you had me and Custis as your witnesses."

"I know the law," she replied. "I've had plenty of run-ins with the law since I was a girl. So I understand what I have to do and how I have to do it before leaving Denver."

"I heard that someone tried to kill you on the way to my office."

"That's right, Doc. And this time, I had a good long look at the man's face."

"Did you recognize him?"

"No. But I will the next time we cross paths."

"Miss," the doctor said, "someone is trying to kill you, so you really should leave Denver."

"I'm going to do just that," Shotgun Sallie told the physician. "But that can wait until tomorrow."

"Why wait?"

"I have a few people to visit," she said, slipping the doctor five dollars. "This is for Bert's care and medicine."

"Thanks." Dr. Potter frowned. "Why are you helping him, a terrible drunk and a complete stranger?"

"Because he believes my name is Samaritan," she said without thinking. "And because I need a good stable hand at my ranch. Someone who loves and understands horses."

"He'll always be a falling-down drunk."

"Not on my ranch, he won't," she promised. "I'll see to that even if I have to have my foreman lock Bert up each and every night while he howls at the moon for his whiskey."

"Hmph," Dr. Potter snorted. "Might work, but I sincerely doubt it. At any rate, I'm going to see Custis after leaving here. Want to come along?"

She shrugged. "What for?"

The doctor pursed his lips in thought and then said, "Because aren't you both looking for the same killers?"

"I believe that we are."

"Then I think it might be wise for you two to hook up. You need Custis and I think he could also use your help."

"I don't require help from anyone, Doc."

"I've heard that line many times before," he replied. "And I always thought it sounded arrogant and wrong-headed. So why don't you come and talk to Custis? He's the best man that I've ever known with a gun. You couldn't find a better man to have at your side in a bad fix or fight."

"I'm not interested because he's a lawman."

"Not anymore, he isn't."

Shotgun Sallie blinked. "You mean that, Doc?"

"I do. Just learned it myself this morning. He resigned his office and turned in his federal officer's badge so that he could go after the men who killed your sister without being shackled by the law."

"Well then," she said, "that sorta changes everything I was thinking and feeling about Custis Long."

"Do you hate lawmen that bad?"

"Almost, Doc. Almost."

"Come along with me," he urged. "You won't be sorry."

"And I've heard that one before," Shotgun Sallie said, unable to hold back a smile. "And it has *always* gotten me in trouble."

Chapter 10

"Custis, you'll be as good as new in a few days," Doc said.

"I'll never be as good as new again, Doc, but thanks for the encouraging words."

Shotgun Sallie looked at Longarm and said, "I heard that you handed in your federal marshal's badge just so that you could be on your own when you hunt my sister's killers."

"That's right."

She frowned and then flopped down in a chair near his bedside. "Maybe I was a little hard on you about my sister's death."

"No, you weren't," Longarm told her. "I deserve all the blame you can dish out."

"But you honestly tried to save her life, didn't you?"

"Of course. However, I'd be lying to you if I said that I was head over heels in love with Lucy. But her death shook me badly. Your sister was one of the nicest women I've ever known . . . not that I'm a real expert on 'nice' women . . . if you catch my drift."

"I catch it. You strike me as a ladies' man, and I'll bet

that most women fall all over themselves trying to catch your eye."

"Your sister didn't. At first, she wanted nothing to do with me."

"And why is that?" Shotgun Sallie asked.

Longarm shrugged. "I expect it was because of my occupation as a lawman and the violence of my past. I've sent a lot of men to the gallows and killed a whole lot more. I've got more sworn enemies than I could shake a stick at."

"And that's why a bunch of them decided to get together and get even, but they killed my sister instead."

"I'm afraid so," Longarm said quietly. "That's about the long and short of it. It was my fault."

"That's true," she said, "but now I'm as much of a target as you are. About an hour ago a man tried to shoot me in the middle of Colfax Avenue."

Longarm sat up straight. "What happened?"

Shotgun Sallie described the event and ended by saying, "I looked right into his face and he was yelling that I was the same as a dead woman. And I *would* be a dead woman if the sonofabitch had been a better shot."

"Did you get a shot off in return?"

"I'd left my shotgun in the barn with Bert, who is in pretty bad shape. It seems that a deputy by the name of Bob Clausen hauled him into an alley last night and nearly beat him to death for the sheer fun of it."

Longarm's lips formed a hard white line. "Deputy Clausen is a vicious and dangerous man. I've talked to his boss, Marshal Oscar Duncan, on several occasions and warned him that Clausen should be stripped of his badge and sent packing."

"I'm leaving Denver tomorrow morning," Shotgun Sallie

said. "But first I'm going to find Clausen and teach him how it feels to suffer *real* pain."

"If you do that, you'll be arrested and thrown in jail," Longarm warned. "Injuring or killing a town marshal is a serious offense. You'll go before a judge and he'll sentence you to spend time in our state prison."

"I can't just let Bob Clausen get away after nearly beating Bert Hollister to death."

"You could," Longarm answered. "But something tells me you won't."

"No, I won't."

Longarm pushed himself out of bed. "I know Deputy Clausen and I know where he likes to hang out in downtown Denver. We can catch him by surprise and teach him a lesson in pain."

"You don't look healthy enough to teach anyone anything," Shotgun Sallie told Longarm.

"I'm tougher than I appear, and I've owed Deputy Clausen a lesson or two for quite some time. To tell you the truth, I'm going to *insist* on administering rough justice to Clausen. There are some men that are so mean or pigheaded that they just can't be reasoned with and have to be taught by force. Clausen falls into that group."

"All right," Shotgun said after a long pause. "Get dressed and let's go find the man and see if he can take it as well as he dishes it out."

It was long after darkness fell when they saw the deputy come strolling out of a saloon. He was a cocky bastard, good-looking and arrogant with the power that he had as a lawman. Longarm and Shotgun Sallie waited in an alley, and when the deputy passed by whistling a tune, they popped a feed sack over his head and dragged him off the sidewalk, kicking and fighting.

Longarm's first punch was an uppercut to Bob Clausen's gut that caused the deputy to gasp and then double up in pain. Shotgun Sallie stepped in and expertly planted the toe of her small boot right between Clausen's legs. The deputy screamed and Longarm gauged where his mouth was and hit him with a straight right cross. There was a loud and familiar popping sound as Clausen's nose broke. Shotgun Sallie somehow found the deputy's ears, grabbed them, and drove her knee up into his face and the man went down sobbing and begging for mercy.

"Don't hurt me anymore! Whoever you are, please don't hurt me anymore!"

"If you're still wearing a badge tomorrow, I'll kill you tomorrow night," Longarm hissed. "You've beaten your last drunk or helpless whore. Do you understand me?"

The feed sack was now blood-soaked from Bob Clausen's broken nose and the man was weeping like a child.

Shotgun Sallie whispered to Longarm, "This man is right-handed, isn't he?"

Longarm nodded.

Shotgun Sallie grabbed the deputy's right hand and, with a sharp twist of her arm, she broke his thumb. Clausen howled and collapsed in the dirt and that's how they left the sorry excuse for a man.

Minutes later they were walking side by side toward Salty's Stables to see Bert. "Shotgun, you play pretty rough. Why, the way you broke that sonofabitch's thumb tells me that you've done that a time or two before tonight."

"I have. It was the second trick I learned when I started out in my trade."

"And the first?" Longarm asked.

"You saw it. I'm even more accurate with the toe of my boot than I am with a shotgun."

"Hope I never get you *really* mad."

"You came close to getting a lot worse than Deputy Clausen," she admitted. "But you were already in pretty tough shape so I held off. Now, I'm going to just let bygones be bygones."

"Thanks."

"Do you think that snake will be scared enough to turn in his badge tomorrow?" Shotgun asked.

"Count on it."

"Good!" She looked up at Longarm. "In that case, I can leave Denver in the morning with Bert."

"You're taking him away?"

"That's right." She stopped in the street. "If he stays here in Denver, Bert Hollister is going to either be beaten to death one of these nights by someone like Clausen or die of alcohol poisoning. The man was a cowboy. He loves horses and I'm betting he's really good with them, so I'm taking him up to my Shotgun Ranch and putting him in charge of all my horses."

"That could be a big mistake," Longarm told her.

"If it is, I'll send him packing," she replied. "But I like Bert and I'm going to give him every chance to get sober and healthy. I know that he might find a bottle and disappoint me but I also know that he'd never harm any of my ranch horses."

"You've got a good heart," Longarm said. "Just like your sister."

"Custis, my heart is made of stone. Lucy's heart was gold. There's really no comparison."

"I think there is," Longarm said. "And what do you think

about my leaving Denver with you and Bert first thing to-morrow morning?"

"Custis, when the man who tried to shoot me down in the street realizes that I've left town, then they're going to come looking for me. And guess where they'll come looking first?"

"Your Shotgun Ranch."

"That's right," she said. "Only, when they come, I'll be on *my* ground and I'll have men to help me."

"If you don't mind, I'd like to come along," Longarm told her. "I sure wouldn't want to miss the reunion you have planned."

"Fair enough."

Longarm's mind was racing. "I'll have to rent a horse and . . ."

"You won't need to do that because I intend to rent a buckboard so that Bert can survive the trip."

"Then everything is settled," Longarm told her.

"Not everything."

"What do you mean?"

Shotgun Sallie actually smiled. "I mean that I don't think it would be wise for either of us to stay in our rooms tonight. It would be better if we slept near Bert to protect him."

"How near do we have to sleep near Bert?"

"Not *too* near," she said, giving him a wink.

Longarm grinned. "Shotgun, that's just what I was hoping you'd say."

Chapter 11

When they got back to Salty's Stables it was pitch-dark inside, so Longarm lit a match and held it up for light. "Bert?"

There was no answer, but they did hear a man snoring. "That will be him," Shotgun guessed. "There's a lantern hanging on a hook over there by that post."

Longarm found the lantern, and after lighting it, he turned it down low. Then he and Shotgun Sallie went over to stand above the slumbering Bert, whose face was battered and badly swollen.

"Clausen really put a beating on poor old Bert," Shotgun Sallie said, not bothering to hide her bitterness.

"Well," Longarm remarked, "Deputy Clausen isn't going to look a whole lot better than Bert right now. I broke his nose and I might even have broken his jaw."

"I hope you did," Shotgun said as she knelt down beside the old cowboy and touched his bruised cheek. "That sonofabitch deserves everything we gave him and more."

"Do you really think that Bert can be moved all the way

up to your ranch?" Longarm asked. "A buckboard is pretty rough riding and Bert looks to be in *terrible* shape."

"He might die on the way up to my Shotgun Ranch, but if he stays here I have a feeling he'll be murdered."

Longarm considered that a moment and then said, "I don't think that Bob Clausen would have the nerve to do that after the beating we gave him."

"I'm not talking about the deputy," Shotgun explained. "I'm talking about the gang that killed my sister and is hell-bent on killing you and me. Don't you imagine that they've been watching us and know about Bert being laid up in this barn?"

"I suspect they might," Longarm agreed.

"And don't you think they'd kill Bert just out of spite?"

"Yeah. They'd do that all right. They might even come for him tonight."

"Then we'll have to take turns staying on guard tonight," Shotgun Sallie said.

"I think you're right about that." Longarm looked around the musty old barn and his eyes landed on a pile of what appeared to be reasonably fresh grass hay. "That pile of horse grass looks almost as comfortable as my own bed," he told her as he walked over to the pile, removed his hat, and stretched out on the grass.

"How is it?"

"Not bad," he replied. "Not bad at all."

She removed her own hat and lay down beside him, but Longarm noted that the woman was keeping her shotgun within reach. "This will do for tonight," she agreed.

For a few minutes they lay side by side, listening to Bert's labored breathing. Longarm wasn't real optimistic that the old cowboy would survive a trip up into the Rockies, but he agreed that there was little choice but to take the risk. If Dr. Potter knew about their plans, he would be in-credulous and flatly refuse to let Bert travel so far in a buckboard, but Longarm knew they'd be out of Denver before Potter got word of their absence.

"Custis?"

"Yeah?"

"I have to ask you something and I want a straight an-swer. No lies. If you lie to me I'll know it and that's the end of things for us."

"What do you want to know?" Longarm asked, although he thought that he could guess.

"Did you and my sister make love on the riverbank just before she was killed?"

Longarm scowled up at the dark and cobwebbed rafters of the barn and considered the consequences of telling her the truth.

"I really need to know," Shotgun Sallie insisted, rolling over onto her side and staring hard at him.

"Yes," he said. "We did. More than once."

She expelled a deep breath and was lost in thought for several minutes. "I guess it's just as well that you did. I had it in my mind that my sister was like . . . like the Virgin Mary or something."

"Your sister was certainly no virgin when I first met her. She was experienced, but she wasn't a loose woman," he said quietly. "She was a bit on the modest side and I liked that. But when we made love, she was pretty free and frisky."

"So she enjoyed it?"

Longarm smiled. "Yes, she did. Very much. And I sure hope that doesn't upset you."

"It . . . it surprises me some. But it doesn't upset me. Matter of fact, I'm glad that you and Lucy made love out there under the sky and by the river. I expect that she was happy just before she was shot."

"She *was* happy," Longarm said, turning on his side so that his face was inches from Shotgun Sallie's face. "And when we made love, I made sure that she was as satisfied by it as I was. I gave her . . . well, I gave her as good as she gave me. There was nothing but giving when we made love. No selfishness and no rush or hurry."

"I . . . I see."

Longarm reached out and his fingers traced her cheekbones, then her lips. "Do you really?"

"Yes."

Her eyes glistened and Longarm realized that she was crying silently; it surprised him because she was so tough and emotionally strong.

"Shotgun, are you sure you're not upset?"

"No. I'm glad. I became a whore at a very early age. I ran away from my family, and a few years later, when I was very sick, I came home and my parents took me back in and nursed me to health. But Lucy was the one who was so kind and forgiving. I had expected our parents to forgive but I thought Lucy would hold it against me for the rest of my life. She didn't and so I put her in a special place in my heart."

"I see."

"There were a few times later on when Lucy needed help. I sent her money and I would have given her everything that I owned, but she never asked for more help than she needed."

"Did she know that you became a madam?" Longarm asked.

"I think so. But we never talked about that. We always talked about good things. Just about flowers and dreams and all that sweet silliness. My sister was the only one I could ever talk to about those kinds of things, and for that I loved her dearly."

"I'm sorry she's gone."

"Me, too. I'll never find anyone that I can talk to like that again."

"Don't be too certain of that."

Shotgun Sallie leaned in and kissed him. It was a gentle kiss, without passion, but even so it stirred Longarm and he brought her into his arms. "I want to make love to you."

"Slow and easy like you did with my sister?"

"If that's what you want, then we'll do it slow and easy."

"I'd rather you make love to me in a different way," she told him. "A little rougher and harder. More like me and less like my sister."

"Whatever you want."

Sallie jumped up and quickly threw off her worn and baggy men's shirt and pants without a trace of modesty. And even though the lantern was turned down low and the light was worse than poor, her body was obviously so lovely that it almost took Longarm's breath away.

She laughed. "Your jaw is hanging open and you look like you just swallowed a horned toad or a hummingbird."

He closed his mouth and said, "I had no idea what was hiding under all those baggy men's clothes. You're a beautiful woman."

"I've been a whore, but I was always picky about who I chose. I never got into the opium or rotgut whiskey like most of the girls. I ate right, exercised, and tried to keep myself clean and healthy."

"Not many whores do that."

"Almost none, although I've been preaching to my girls about staying healthy and clean. I've seen too many girls end up sick and dying even before they were yet out of their late twenties." She glanced toward the entrance to the barn and said, "I wonder where the fella who owns this barn sleeps at night. His name is Salty?"

"Yes," Longarm answered, "but Salty died last winter. His brother took over this stable but the man doesn't like the business and so he stays away. The brother is worthless and he hopes that old Bert will keep the stable open and running until it's sold."

"Well, after tonight, he's going to have to find another Bert," she said with conviction, "because Bert is about to take up a whole new life on my horse and cattle ranch. But never mind about that right now. Custis, stand up and let me see what you got hanging between those long legs of yours."

Longarm undressed almost as fast as Shotgun Sallie, and when they were standing face to face, she took his manhood in both of her hands and gently massaged the head of his tool with the tip of her fingers until he was as hard as a hickory stick.

"You're big," she said, looking into his eyes with amusement and no small amount of budding desire.

"Glad I meet with your approval. How about we stop talking and get down to some serious screwing?"

"How do you like it?" she asked, kneeling down on the grass and tickling the tip of his tool with her tongue.

"That's pretty good for starters." He gulped.

"If you think this feels good, then wait until we get to the finish," she told him as she took his rod into her mouth and began to do things better than any woman he'd ever known.

Minutes later, Longarm was on top of Shotgun Sallie and he was taking her rough and ready, just like she'd requested. Her legs were long and shapely and she had wrapped them around his waist. Longarm was plunging and she was bucking and their grunts and gasps drowned out Bert's loud snoring.

"Come on!" she urged. "Deeper! Faster and faster!"

Longarm gave her everything he had and the harder he pumped, the better she seemed to like it. Her face was ringed by the grass hay, and wisps of it had somehow slipped between her big, heaving breasts. Their breathing came faster and faster and Longarm was pistoning like a steam engine and she was laughing and whooping with pleasure.

"Oh gawd, yes!" she cried, crushing him with her arms and legs as her body began to jerk and thrust wildly upward.

Longarm growled like a dog over a fresh bone and then he took her lunging and pounding in an orgy of passion that seemed to go on and on.

"What time is it?" she asked after she rolled off a thoroughly exhausted and well-satisfied Longarm.

"My pocket watch is in my vest pocket," he panted. "How many times have we screwed since we got here?"

"I lost count," Shotgun Sallie admitted. "Three or four. You up for another romp before daybreak?"

"I need some water and food to eat."

"You ate me," Shotgun Sallie reminded him with a devilish grin. "I gave you dessert."

"Yeah, you did." He laughed. "But a man needs something to sink his teeth into and I don't think you'd have been too happy if I'd have done that to your . . . dessert."

"No, I wouldn't have," she agreed as she found his pocket watch and walked over to the low-burning lantern.

"It's almost four o'clock in the morning. There won't be any cafés open yet."

"In Denver there's always someplace to get food, drink, or a woman," he told her. "In fact, there's a café just up the street that's open all night. They get a lot of drunks coming out of the saloons and all the insomniacs. I've eaten there many a dark morning waiting for dawn."

"I'm pretty hungry myself," she admitted.

"Then let's get dressed and go have a big breakfast and a pot of strong coffee," he suggested. "We're going to have to eat something before we leave Denver or we'll soon be famished."

"All right. What about your things at your apartment?"

He hadn't even given packing for the trip a thought yet. "Well," he said, "there are some things that I really need to bring along since I plan to be gone awhile. I've got a good Winchester rifle and a box of ammunition. I'll need extra clothes and I have a few other things I'd like to grab and take with us to your ranch."

"Tell you what," Shotgun Sallie said. "Let's get dressed and then eat. After that you go to your apartment, pack up your belongings, and meet me back here at this barn. By then I'll have hitched up a horse and that buckboard I saw out back and we'll be gone about sunup."

"What about payment to Salty's brother?" he asked. "We can't just steal one of his horses."

"Spoken like a dyed in the wool lawman," she said with a mocking smile. "Custis, I rode in on a good saddle horse, but I doubt it will accept a harness. It's a fine animal and I'll just swap her for one of Salty's harness horses and leave enough in cash to make up for the wagon and harness. I figure a hundred dollars and my saddle horse in trade will be more than fair."

"I expect it will be. If I remember right, the buckboard is in almost as bad shape as this falling-down old livery barn. When Salty used to rent the buckboard out, he hitched it to a dapple gray gelding."

"I know the one you're talking about and that's the one I'll take." Sallie began to dress. "Let's get to moving, Custis. I sure want to have eaten and gotten out of Denver before it wakes up and maybe some eyes that we don't want watching see us leaving."

"All right," he said, starting to get dressed. "It sounds like as good a plan as any."

"We'll have to leave Bert alone while we're at the café," she said, glancing toward the sleeping cowboy. "You think that's going to be all right?"

"Yes. Bert will be fine."

"He'd better be," Shotgun Sallie said as she reached for her hat and then her faithful shotgun.

Chapter 12

They ate a hearty breakfast with a sleepy-eyed cook watching from behind his stove.

"More coffee, gravy, and biscuits!" Longarm called out to the cook. "And I'll take another slab of ham."

"Coming up," the cook said without a trace of enthusiasm.

Across the table from Longarm, Shotgun Sallie stretched and said, "What a night we had! Do I look as tired as I feel?"

"You looked good in lamplight on a pile of grass hay, and you still look good," Longarm said with complete honesty.

"I feel like I've been run over by a herd of cattle," she admitted.

Longarm brushed back his handlebar mustache. "Are you already complaining about our lovemaking?"

"No," she said, warming him with a weary smile. "I'm not complaining at all. We were very, very good together."

"You've got wisps of hay in your hair and the cook might be getting suspicious about where we've come from."

Shotgun Sallie looked over at the cook, leaned across

the table, and said, "To be truthful, I don't think he's even fully awake, much less curious about the night we spent on a pile of grass screwing our brains out."

"You might be right about that," Longarm conceded, lowering his voice as the chubby and bleary-eyed cook waddled over with a pot of coffee to refill their cups.

"Ain't seen you in a while, Marshal Long," the cook said, wiping his greasy hands on a dirty apron. "Thought maybe someone finally punched you a one-way ticket to the cemetery."

"Not yet, George. And I've resigned from the marshal's office, so now I'm just Custis."

"You *resigned*?" George said, with genuine surprise. "Why, Marshal, you can't do that!"

"I already did. I'm a civilian now."

"How are you goin' to make a livin'? Jobs are kinda tough to find these days."

"I'm leaving town for a while. Going to move up to this lady's Shotgun Ranch near Central City."

"Is that a fact?" George looked closer at Shotgun Sallie, saw the grass in her hair and the flush on her cheeks, and finally made all the mental connections. "Why, that's real nice! But we'll miss having you around, Marshal. It just won't be the same in Denver if we don't read about you killin' some deserving jackass now and again."

"Maybe not, George, but sometimes a man has to make a few changes in his life."

George nodded with all three of his chins. "I'd like to quit this damn job and do something easier. I don't make much money for havin' to stay up all night and deal with drunks and whores."

"What would you like to do if you weren't a cook?" Longarm asked with idle curiosity.

George actually chuckled, something that Longarm had never seen the man do even once in all the visits he'd made to this café. Then the fat man said, "I'd like to be a United States Marshal just like you!"

It was all that Longarm could do not to choke on his coffee. "No kiddin'?"

"I'm serious. Since you quit maybe you could even put a good word in for me at the Federal Building so I could take your place."

Across the table, Shotgun Sallie was having trouble holding down her laughter.

"Will ya, Marshal?"

"Well, I dunno," Longarm said, trying to keep a straight face. "George, can you shoot to kill?"

"Shoot a man?"

"Marshals and lawmen don't go around shooting dogs and cats, George. Wearing a badge makes you a target for anyone that ever had a grudge against a lawman. Doesn't matter if the grudge is aimed specifically against you or at some other fella who maybe threw them in jail or busted their noggin' with the butt of his gun. Either way, once you pin on a badge, then you're a target, and to be honest, you're a pretty big one."

George looked down at his protruding gut. "Yeah, I see what you mean. And I don't know if I could shoot to kill a man or not."

"George, I think you'd better be looking for some other profession."

"Maybe so," he said, "but I can't do anything but cook."

"Then I guess you'd better stick it out," Longarm told the man.

George suddenly lifted his nose like a dog sniffing scent. "Oh, shit!" he cried. "My ham is burning on the stove!"

"I'll take it burned," Longarm yelled at the cook as the man raced for his kitchen.

"Custis," Shotgun Sallie said, "I'm stuffed. I've had enough coffee to float a barge so I'll be going back to Salty's and getting that dapple gray hitched to the buckboard. Daylight is coming soon and I'd sure like to be gone."

"Me, too," he said, lowering his voice. "I expect you noticed that I told George where we were going after we left Denver."

"I did."

"George is a good fella but he has a loose tongue. He'll tell people where we're heading and I'm sure that the word will get to the ones that we want to come gunning."

"So we've used ourselves to bait the hook," she said, coming to her feet. "See you soon at Salty's."

"Right. I'll just wolf down another slice of ham and a cup of coffee and be out this door in ten minutes. I'll meet you back at Salty's with my bag in less than forty-five minutes."

"We'll be ready to roll by then. I'll just need you to help me get Bert into the buckboard."

"Good enough," Longarm said as the woman left the café.

Shotgun Sallie really had to pee because of all the coffee she'd consumed. She hurried across the street and walked as fast as she could to Salty's Stables and then she rounded the barn with her shotgun in her hands and went into the darkness where she could pee in private.

It felt so damned good to pee when your bladder was about to burst, and she just kept going and going. When she was finished, she hitched her baggy pants back up and was about to reach for her shotgun when two men rushed her in the darkness. Shotgun Sallie let out a cry and kicked at one of the men. She felt the toe of her boot hit something hard and then she was falling with a man on top of her. A second later, she felt powerful hands tighten on her neck. Gasping, clawing, and fighting for her life, she felt a fist crash into her temple and lost consciousness as she spiraled down into a pit of pain and darkness.

She awoke in Salty's barn, bound hand and foot. Two men were standing over her, and when Shotgun Sallie tried to yell, she discovered that they had gagged her.

"Ain't this a real bucket of pig shit?" one of the men said laughingly with his arms folded across his broad chest.

Shotgun Sallie's eyes blazed as she glared up at the pair. One of them was the same man who had recently tried to gun her down on Colfax Avenue. She could see the first light of day creeping through the barn door, and when she turned her head to the side, she saw Bert lying on the floor also bound and gagged.

"Is your big friend, Marshal Custis Long, coming back to screw you a few more times?" the red-haired man taunted.

Shotgun tried to cuss the sonofabitch out, but it was a futile effort so she just hissed through the gag.

"Maybe Otis and me will have a few turns humpin' you," the other man said, speaking for the first time in a voice pitched with excitement.

They both cackled lewdly, and that made Shotgun Sallie's blood boil.

"Hank, we'd better get ready to greet Custis Long. I expect he'll be coming back here at any time for another poke at her."

"I'd sure like to hump her right now."

"It'll have to wait. After we kill the marshal we'll flip a

coin to see who gets to mount Shotgun Sallie first. We'll tie her ankles to a three-foot-long board and do it to her until she smokes."

"Yeah!" Hank said, his voice hoarse with desire. "And we'd better use our knives on all three of 'em when we're finished so nobody from town comes a-runnin'."

"Either that or take 'em out of town bound and gagged and then go up in the mountains to join the rest of the clan and kill 'em real slow. That way we can bury their bodies and no one will ever be the wiser."

"Otis," Hank said, spitting tobacco on the ground, "sometimes you really surprise me."

"How so?"

"Well, just out of the blue you come up with somethin' so smart that I realize you ain't totally stupid."

"Thanks a hell of a lot," Otis growled.

Longarm had a satchel in one hand and his Winchester in the other as he walked briskly up Colfax toward Salty's Stables. He was tired from the lack of sleep, but he felt good and his mind was fully occupied on the changes he'd made in his life. Handing in his badge had been a huge decision, and he wondered if his boss, Billy Vail, had even put in the paperwork to certify his resignation. Probably not. But Longarm had resigned and so he was now on his own and he wondered if the killers would come after them. If they did, Longarm knew that he, Shotgun Sallie, and Bert Hollister wouldn't be able to outrun them in a buckboard.

Well, Longarm thought as he neared Salty's Stables just as the sun was coming up in the east, *we've upped the ante in this deadly game and now let's let the cards fall where they may and see what happens.*

Chapter 13

Longarm stepped inside Salty's old barn and squinted to see better through the darkness. "Shotgun?" he called. "Bert?"

The hammer of a gun clicked behind him, and before Longarm could drop the satchel and swing his rifle upward, he felt a terrible pain explode in his head and he went down to his knees. Trying to stay conscious, he fought to get to his feet but when he was halfway erect a boot caught him in the stomach and knocked him sprawling.

Longarm rolled and fumbled for the gun on his hip but another boot lashed out and his gun went sailing. Then two men landed on him with fists and feet, and Longarm, already dazed, passed out.

When he awoke, he was tied hand and foot, gagged and lying between Shotgun Sallie and Bert Hollister in the back of a buckboard. Longarm looked up saw the sun straight overhead. There were no buildings around them, so he knew that they had already left downtown Denver far behind. And even with his head pounding with pain, he could see that they were moving in a westerly direction up into the mountains.

Otis glanced back over his shoulder with Sallie's shotgun cradled in his dirty hands. "You enjoyin' the ride, Marshal Long? Hope you and the woman and that old drunk are all havin' a real good time. 'cause by this time tomorrow you're going to be pushing up rocks and dirt."

Otis cackled and the other big man who was driving the buckboard burst into insane laughter. Longarm looked up at their taunting and brutish faces and saw that they were both redheads, and he wondered where they were taking him and if there would be others waiting to carry out their twisted revenge.

He tried to say something, but the gag made that impossible so he rolled his head and looked at Shotgun Sallie, whose eyes were wide open. With most any other woman he would have expected to see fear, but that certainly was not the case with this Shotgun Sallie, whose eyes were filled with anger and an intense burning ferocity.

Bert Hollister, on the other hand, looked nearly dead and his eyes were closed. Because he was so beaten and weak, they hadn't even bothered to tie up his hands or feet.

"Up ahead is a nice place to pull over by the river," Otis told his brother. "We can pull into them trees and rest the gray."

"It could go a while longer," Hank said. "When we start pullin' up the steep grades, I'm goin' to have to figure a way to harness either my horse or yours to this buckboard. We're too heavy a load for one animal to pull, and the dapple we stole ain't that big or strong."

"My horse won't do 'er," Otis replied. "He'll wreck this wagon before he allows himself to be put in harness."

"I think my horse will pull if I can rig up a harness out of my saddle leather."

"If you do that it'll look pretty ridiculous and attract attention, which is the last thing we need with those three tied up in back."

"You're right," Hank said after a long pause. "Well, we can't pull this mountain grade with all this weight so I guess we'll just have to lighten the load a mite."

"What are you thinkin'?" Otis asked.

Hank glanced over his shoulder into Longarm's eyes and said, "The marshal man swam away from us after we shot his woman by the South Platte River. I reckon today we'll see if he can swim when he's full of lead. Same for the old stable hand drunk."

"And after we kill them two we can take Shotgun Sallie up to meet our whole family," Otis said, his voice filling with excitement. "We tell our kinfolk how she blew off our brother's head and then we let everybody have a time to get even with her."

"That's right! Anybody who wants to can do what they'd like with Shotgun Sallie. By the time they get done with her, she'll be beggin' for mercy and wantin' to die."

"I think that's a fine idea!"

Longarm heard all this and knew that his time as well as that of Bert Hollister was almost up unless he somehow quickly figured out a way to either escape or kill this pair. They had taken Longarm's sidearm and Winchester, but by moving his upper arm along his side he suddenly realized he still had that little two-shot derringer that was cleverly attached to his watch fob. And that pistol now seemed like his only hope.

The passage of time felt to Longarm like an eternity while the brothers drove the buckboard off the mountain road toward a killing place. The rickety old wagon noisily bounced and jostled through a small meadow deep into the riverside seclusion of heavy aspen and pines. Longarm could hear the sound of rushing water and the grunts of Shotgun Sallie as she struggled furiously to untie herself. Unfortunately, Otis and Hank were good with ropes, and try as they might, Longarm wasn't making much headway getting his hands free, and he was sure the same could be said for Shotgun Sallie.

"This will do just fine," Hank said as the wagon came to a halt. "Nobody can see us from the road, and the river along this stretch of the canyon is deep and fast."

Longarm was working furiously at the ropes that bound his hands behind his back and he was sweating even though the day was cool and the canyon was draped in shadow. The roar of the river told him that even if he survived bullets, he probably would be torn and battered to death if they tossed him into the swift water.

"I sure got to piss real bad!" Hank said, jumping down from the buckboard. "We got any food to eat?"

"You know we don't. Forgot to get it in town but there's a few saloons and stores along the road up ahead where we can get something to eat. I did find a bottle of good whiskey in the marshal's bag."

"Then I reckon we'll survive just fine," Hank said. "Get the bottle while I take a piss and tie up the horses."

"All right."

Longarm had just managed to chew through his gag and now he urgently whispered to Shotgun Sallie. "There's a two-shot derringer in my vest pocket attached to my watch fob and chain. It's on my left side. If I roll your way, can you dig it out with your hands still tied behind your back?"

Her face was inches from his own and she both grunted and nodded.

"Good! It's our only hope. If you can get it out of my

pocket, one of us has to get it aimed from behind our backs and shoot these bastards."

Again, she nodded in assent, so Longarm rolled over and bumped up tight against her back and hissed, "See if you can get it out of my vest pocket. Hurry up!"

He felt her fumbling at his vest pocket and knew that with her wrists tied just as tightly as his own, Shotgun Sallie's fingers would be completely numb from lack of circulation. On top of that, even if she could manage to manipulate the derringer and fire off both rounds, it was highly unlikely that she could do it with any accuracy.

Longarm leaned in even closer, and after what seemed like an eternity, he felt the derringer being lifted from his pocket.

"You got it!" he whispered. "Pull out the watch and chain, too! Pull it all out so that they won't see it until it's too late."

Shotgun Sallie was grunting and straining to do as he asked. After at least a full minute and maybe even longer, she stopped struggling. "Got it all free?"

"Uh-huh!"

"Can you get your finger on the trigger and hold the derringer tight?"

Again, she nodded, her chin digging into his shoulder.

Otis leaned over the buckboard. "Marshal, it's time for you and Bert to stretch your legs."

The buckboard had low sides and a short back gate just high enough to have kept them hidden. Now Hank dropped the gate on its rusty hinges and grabbed Longarm by his boots.

"Otis, give me a hand. This bastard is heavy."

A moment later, Otis and Hank pulled Longarm off the buckboard. He dropped heavily on his side and they rolled him onto his back. "Marshal, do you think you can show us how well you can swim with your hands and feet tied?"

"Go to hell," Longarm snarled.

"Well, look at that!" Hank said, drawing his gun. "The big, bad marshal has done chewed his gag off and he's wanting to say good-bye."

"Get him on his feet and we can set him on that rock by the water and take target practice."

"Shoot him full of holes and let our bullets knock him over backward into the water. I like that," Hank said. "I have always wanted to see if I could shoot the ears off a lawman from ten paces."

"Bet you can't."

"Bet I can!"

Longarm growled. "You boys are having your fun now, but if you kill me you'll be hunted down like dogs. You and however many others of you are still left among your clan."

"Save your breath, Marshal Long. 'Cause after we shoot off your ears and then put a few lead pills in your guts, you're going to need your breath in that cold river."

"Why don't you let the woman and Bert go?" Longarm said, desperate to buy time as he watched Shotgun Sallie sit up in the buckboard and then try to turn around so she could aim the derringer in the direction of the brothers. Longarm could see the desperation in her movements and he realized that she wasn't going to be of any help. The derringer was a short-range pistol, and even if Shotgun Sallie had her hands free and was composed, making two kills at the existing distance between her and the brothers would have been a miraculous stroke of luck.

"Sit him on that rock right there by the water," Otis said, grunting with exertion. "That's the way." He stepped back and winked. "Now, Marshal Long, I want you to sit up real straight like you was having your picture taken by a photographer for posterity."

"Sod you."

Otis stepped forward and backhanded Longarm across the face, knocking him back on the rock and almost causing him to topple into the river. And for an instant, Longarm thought that would have been his only chance, but when he saw the white foaming current churning just a few feet below, he knew that with his limbs tied he would have had no chance at all.

"Now sit up and lift your chin," Hank ordered, as he drew out his pistol. "I want to shoot the left ear clean off. If I miss and hit you in the head, though, I have to say that I won't be all that sorry."

Otis tilted back the bottle of whiskey, drank hard, and giggled with the liquor running down his square chin. "Hank, this is pretty good whiskey! Maybe we ought to take our time havin' our fun."

Hank grabbed the bottle from his brother and took a long pull. He choked, and when he spoke his voice was raw. "That *is* good whiskey! Mighty nice of you to have bought the good stuff for us to enjoy, Marshal."

Longarm knew that they were playing with him, having their fun. He had seen cats tease half-dead mice this way and he understood their minds. He also understood that every minute they drank, laughed, and tormented him was another minute he had left to live and hope for a miracle.

"Say, Marshal, how was that woman you had by the river the day we came upon you? She looked real juicy. Too bad she took the bullet meant for you. We'd have enjoyed having our pleasure on her."

"Do your brothers live close by here?" Longarm asked. "I'll bet you come from an inbred family. Is that right?"

"You'll never know," Otis scoffed, "because you'll be feeding fish."

"Before you kill me, I'd like to know who you are and what I did that made your family come for me. I really don't recall seeing either of your ugly faces."

"You never have. You never saw any of us brothers," Hank said before upending the bottle and taking a quick drink. "But you made our mammy a widow woman about six years ago up in these mountains."

"What was your father's name?" Longarm persisted.

Otis and Hank exchanged glances and then Otis said, "I guess it don't hurt anymore to tell you. Our pa's name was Kenyon Fernow. That's who we are, the Fernow boys, and there are eight of us altogether. I'm Otis, eldest son of Kenyon, and this here is the next in line, Hank."

"What was the name of the one that I killed at the Drury Stables?"

"That would be Corlis. And the woman in the wagon went and blew off our brother Melvin's head. He was Ma's favorite, 'cause he was the handsomest, though she says we are all exceptional-lookin' boys."

"You're all a bunch of bloody assholes, is what you are," Longarm said forcing a cold smile. "And now that you have refreshed my memory, I remember your father. Kenyon Fernow was smaller than you boys and he was a cowardly backshooter."

"You shut up about our pa!" Otis cried, dragging out his pistol and unleashing a shot that missed Longarm by inches.

Longarm was trying not to watch what was going on in the buckboard. But suddenly he saw Bert Hollister sit straight up and the derringer was in the old cowboy's shaking hands. Beside him, Shotgun Sallie was trying to ease off the end of the buckboard, and even though her hands were still tied behind her back, there was no doubt that she fully intended to charge the brothers and maybe hope to knock them down into the river.

"You got any last thing to say, Marshal Long?" Otis asked.

"Only that I'd like to die with my ears on. But since you're standing so close, I guess that's not going to happen. You boys must be terrible shots if you can't back up and make a good shot or two."

"I'm a damn good shot!" Otis swore, backing up and taking a pull on the bottle.

"What about you, Hank? Or are you going to stand close enough that anyone could shoot off my ears?"

Hank retreated a half dozen steps, yelling, "I sure don't mind if I miss and put one through your eye, Marshal!"

Longarm lifted his chin and stared at them as they took turns drinking from his whiskey and not at all realizing that Bert Hollister had come alive enough to raise and attempt to aim the derringer that Shotgun Sallie had passed on to him in the buckboard. The cowboy eased closer, dangling his legs off the tailgate, and Longarm saw him take a long, deep breath and square his thin shoulders.

"Hey, *shit heads*," Bert said quietly.

The brothers whirled around, and that's when the old cowboy shot them both at almost point-blank range.

Otis must have taken his bullet through the heart; he fell backward with a scream, kicking his heels against the grass and dirt. Hank Fernow took his bullet just under the collarbone. The slug spun him around and he staggered toward Longarm, fighting to lift his gun.

Longarm threw himself off the rock, took two hops, and drove his shoulder into Hank, knocking him headlong into the roaring white water. For a moment Longarm saw the man's terrified face surface and then the swift river swallowed Hank and he was gone.

Longarm tumbled to the ground and Bert dropped the derringer and walked unsteadily over to his side. "You all right, Marshal?"

"Nice work, Bert. Now find a knife and cut us loose."

"Sure will," Bert said, eyeing the whiskey bottle that was spilling out the last of its contents into the dirt. "But can't let that good whiskey go to waste, can I?"

Longarm choked in exasperation. "Bert, dammit, get a knife!"

But the old cowboy just smiled at him and retrieved the bottle. There wasn't much left inside, but what there was Bert drained with obvious relish. When the bottle was empty, he smacked his lips, tossed the empty into the river, and then he knelt over Otis, searching for a pocketknife. He found one and then he wobbled over to Shotgun Sallie.

"Ladies first," he chuckled. "And besides that, she's my *boss.*"

With a shaking hand, he first cut the bonds around her ankles and then the ones that held her hands behind her back.

"You all right, Miss?" he asked.

She tore at the gag, pulling and spitting it away. Then Shotgun Sallie looked at Bert and said, "I already warned you that you can't drink and work for me."

"Sorry, ma'am. Wasn't but a drop or two left in that bottle. Couldn't let it go waste, could I?"

For a moment, they looked deeply into each other's eyes and then Shotgun Sallie smiled, reached out, and patted Bert on the shoulder. "No, I guess you couldn't at that. Nice work, cowboy."

"My pleasure, Miss Shotgun."

Together, they walked over to Longarm and untied him without a word being spoken until Longarm said, "Bert, you did well hitting both men with my derringer. I didn't think an old cowboy could shoot a derringer that straight."

"They were standing right there in front of me, Marshal. Hard to miss them being so close and both being so big."

"Even so," Longarm said, "your good shooting saved our lives."

"That's right," Shotgun Sallie told the shaky old cowboy. "And now we know who is after us and why."

"The Fernow Clan," Longarm said. "They're legendary in the small towns and settlements scattered throughout the Rockies. I don't know how many there are but I've never heard a good word about any of them."

"They're thicker than ticks on a dying dog," Shotgun Sallie said. "And like most of the clans from the Great Smoky Mountains that moved westward, they hold their honor as dearly as blood."

"So I guess that we've got our work cut out for us if we intend to go on living," Longarm said.

Shotgun Sallie said, "I'd say that we're in a hell of a mess. The Fernow Clan isn't going to quit coming for us until we are dead."

Longarm rubbed at the raw places on his wrists and then turned to stare at the dead man. "We'll try to make our peace with the clan," he said, "but if that doesn't work, then we'll just have to kill them to the last man."

Shotgun Sallie grimly nodded in total agreement.

Chapter 14

They had searched a few hundred yards down the river but there had been no sign of Hank Fernow's body, so they'd loaded up Otis and headed back down to Denver.

"The first thing we'll do is drop Otis off at the Heaven's Door Funeral Parlor," Longarm said. "Then we'll return the wagon to Salty's and get everything straightened out before we leave again."

"Are you going to see the local marshal and report what happened up on the river?" Shotgun Sallie asked as Longarm reined the exhausted dapple gray gelding up in front of the funeral parlor.

"I'd better do that as well as make a call on my old boss, Billy Vail, just to let him know what is happening and who was behind the killings."

"All right," she replied. "I'm going to take Bert by to see Doc Potter. I know he'll be mad enough at us to bite railroad spikes in half for taking him out of town."

"Bert?" Longarm called as he climbed down from the buckboard. "Don't tell anyone that it was *you* that shot Hank and Otis Fernow to death."

"Why not?" the cowboy asked with a puzzled expression on his bruised face. "I'm damned proud of what I done. Hell, I'm prouder of doin' that than I have been of anything I've done in years!"

"And you should be proud," Longarm told him. "But the Fernow Clan is already after both my and Shotgun Sallie's heads. I can't imagine you'd want those boys to take a blood oath to also kill you."

Bert thought about that for a moment and said, "Don't matter what kind of a damned oath those bastards take against me. If they're bound and determined to kill the both of you, then they'll also have to kill me. We're all in this together, ain't we?"

"We are for a fact," Shotgun Sallie told him. "But all the same I think it would be best if you let Custis take the credit for putting down Hank and Otis Fernow."

"Oh, all right," Bert reluctantly agreed. "But I ain't afraid of them Fernow boys. I killed two of 'em and I can kill a few more if necessary."

"You need to remember that *I* killed them," Longarm told the cowboy. "Bert, do I have your word that's what everyone in this town is going to hear before we leave for the Shotgun Ranch?"

"I reckon, Marshal."

"Good." He looked up at Shotgun Sallie, who had slid over and taken up the reins. "I expect that you'll need to get your saddle horse and find a fresh pair to pull this buckboard all the way up to your ranch near Central City."

"I will do that directly. But first I need to buy a load of supplies, and that's definitely going to make two harness horses necessary."

"I'll meet you at Salty's in a few hours," Longarm told her. "Until then, be on your guard. There may be a few Fernow men still in Denver, and when they learn that we killed Otis and Hank, they'll go crazy."

Bert had taken Otis's six-gun and holster and strapped it to his side. "I'll watch over her, Marshal."

"I'm not a marshal anymore, Bert."

"You'll always be Marshal Long to me," Bert argued. "Now get that stinkin' Fernow carcass into the funeral parlor and let's take care of business and get out of this damned town. Denver has been hard luck for me for way too many years."

Longarm dragged Otis's body out of the back of the buckboard. It had bled out completely; Bert had gotten soaked with bloodstains and the old cowboy was pretty upset about that fact. Longarm and Shotgun Sallie had agreed that they should buy Bert some fresh clothes and even a pair of decent cowboy boots before they left for the ranch.

An hour later Longarm was through filling in local marshal Oscar Duncan about the gunfight and giving him the details of the deaths of the Fernow brothers. Marshal Duncan was not pleased, and as Longarm was leaving, he said, "You killed Hank and Otis Fernow and you're going to set off a gawdamn war in my town!" the local marshal exclaimed in anger.

Longarm stopped at the door on his way out and turned to face the agitated lawman. "Duncan," he said, "you're not worth spit. Your man Bob Clausen was a disgrace to the field of law enforcement, and despite my repeated warnings, you never did a damn thing about reining in the vicious bastard."

·"And I have absolutely no doubt that *you* are the one who put a sack over Bob's head and beat him half senseless and made him so afraid that he turned in his badge!"

"I'm not saying that I did . . . and I'm not saying that I didn't," Longarm replied. "But I am mighty glad to hear that Bob Clausen is seeking another line of work in Denver."

"He *left* Denver like a scalded dog! You beat him up so badly that he was shaking with fear and he couldn't even speak right because you broke not only his damned nose but also his jaw."

"Bob got what was coming to him, and whoever beat him up did you a favor, only you're too stupid to realize that fact."

"Get the hell out of my town," the marshal growled. "And don't come back."

"Oh, I'll be back," Longarm promised. "And maybe I'll run against you one of these days and put some respect back in this office. And, if that don't sit right in your craw, why don't you just do something about it right now?"

Duncan shook his finger at Longarm and shouted, "I ought to arrest you, is what I ought to do!"

Longarm raised his fists. "Try it and see what happens, Oscar. Please throw just one lousy punch so I can kick your cowardly ass so far down the street a bloodhound couldn't find it. Why, you're so crooked you have to screw on your damned socks, and on top of that you're as lacking in truth as a goat is in feathers. Come on and fight, you sorry sack of chicken shit!"

Marshal Duncan's face turned beet red with anger, but he didn't dare move or say another word until Longarm turned and disgustedly slammed the door in his wake.

Then minutes later Longarm was at the Federal Building, stomping into Billy Vail's office and interrupting a staff meeting.

Billy took one look at Longarm's grim and angry face and said to his staff members, "Let's take a break. I need to talk to Marshal Long in private."

Custis ground his teeth in silence until the room emptied and they were alone. "Billy, haven't you told everyone that I resigned and handed in my badge?"

"Nope." Billy opened his top desk drawer and placed Longarm's badge on the desk in plain view. "Are you ready to pin it back on?"

"I can't," Longarm said, going on to explain what had happened in the last twenty-four hours since he, Shotgun Sallie, and Bert had been bound hand and foot and tossed into the back of a buckboard on a one-way trip to eternity.

"So it was the Fernow Clan behind all these killings?"

"That's right. But I don't know who actually killed Miss Lucy Coyle out on the South Platte River that afternoon that we had our picnic." Longarm's shoulders sagged and he wearily dropped into one of Billy's leather office chairs and kicked his long legs out in front of him. "Before Otis died, he told me that his father was Kenyon Fernow. Remember that sonofabitch?"

"Of course. You tracked down that bushwhacker up near Granite Creek and shot him after he tried to ambush you."

"That's right. Kenyon was a worthless weasel, but he was also cunning and dangerous. For a few years he had half the people up near Granite Creek scared out of their wits of him and his boys, who all turned out to be just as cruel and deadly as their old man. I never quite knew how many sons Kenyon had and I never cared until now."

"Do you know how many there are left?"

Longarm replied, "Otis admitted to having seven brothers. There were eight altogether. The one I shot in Drury

Stables was Corlis. The one whose head Shotgun Sallie blew off was Melvin, and now Hank and Otis are dead. That means that four are dead and four are left."

"Custis, I think that you should take a few of my federal officers, go up toward Granite Creek or wherever they are to be found, and arrest the bunch of them. They're worse than a snake pit full of vipers and twice as poisonous. And they won't stop until you, Shotgun Sallie, and old Bert are dead."

"What evidence would we have to arrest and then get a conviction against any of them?" Longarm bluntly asked. "The four remaining Fernow brothers sure aren't going to admit to being there when Lucy Coyle was murdered along the South Platte River. And besides that, the Fernow Clan is strung out all over the mountains. Once we arrest the four remaining brothers, the others will come out of the woodwork and there will be a vendetta, and nobody wants that to happen."

"So," Billy said, leaning forward, "what are you going to do? Just wait until the remaining four brothers and however many other members of that despicable clan gather and come for your bloody scalp?"

"What else can I do?" Longarm asked. "Shotgun Sallie has a ranch up near Central City. I haven't asked her but I gather she has at least four or five loyal ranch hands."

"Ranch hands aren't going to be a match against the Fernow men bent on revenge."

"Maybe; maybe not. All I know is that we are leaving Denver and going up to her ranch, and then we'll see what happens. If I can find out who heads the clan now, then I'll try to get a message to him and settle the feud. If I can't, then we'll just wait and take them on when they come gunning for us."

"If you do that, it would really help things if the law was on your side," Billy said. "And by that I mean you wearing your federal marshal's badge."

"Billy, I just can't drag you and this office into this gathering firestorm. I can't. And more important, I *won't*."

Billy sighed and leaned back in his chair. "I don't like the odds that you, Shotgun Sallie, and her boys are setting yourselves up against. Don't like them a bit."

"You know that Shotgun Sallie and I won't be easy pickin's," Longarm said, managing a smile. "We can take care of ourselves, and maybe there are some good shooters up at her ranch."

"So you won't take on your badge?"

"I just can't, but thanks for the offer."

"Will you come back to Denver and put it on if you survive the Fernow men?"

"I think so. A few minutes ago I had a bad time with Marshal Oscar Duncan. After I dropped Otis Fernow's body off at the funeral parlor I knew that I had to pay him an official visit, but he's rotten to the core and I told him to his face that I just might run for local office and put him out of his job."

"Ha!" Billy cried. "Why would you want to do that and take a pay cut as well as have to deal with the damn town council and all the city politics that go with that stinking job?"

"Maybe I just want to see the man out of office. I could win and then resign after I find an honest and competent replacement, couldn't I?"

Billy put Longarm's badge back into his top drawer and said, "I suppose."

"Billy, I've got to go now. We'll be leaving for the Shotgun Ranch right away. Before very long I intend to see you again, when this Fernow mess is all put to rest."

"Put to rest in a graveyard is how it's going to end up and we both know that."

"I suppose we do."

"Custis?"

He turned back to his boss and friend. "What?"

"I'd take a leave of absence from this job if you want me to stand by you up there against the Fernow men."

"I know you'd do that," Longarm said, genuinely moved by the man's offer. "But you have a family and a career here, and the federal government needs honest and good men like you to run things."

"All right."

Longarm stepped back up to Billy's desk, opened his humidor, and removed five excellent and expensive Cuban cigars. "But I will take these for good luck and my pleasure, if you don't mind."

"I *do* mind but take them anyway," Billy said, grinning. "And when you come back I'll have you buy me a steak dinner in return."

"Deal," Longarm said, stuffing one of the Cuban cigars in his mouth and the other four in his front coat pocket.

Less than an hour later, he was back at Salty's wearing a fresh suit and shave.

"Aren't you looking fine," Shotgun Sallie said. "Too bad that Bert and I are dusty and dirty and stink to high heaven."

"Maybe you could take a swim in the river with me tonight," he suggested.

"Not in that river! I won't soon forget how it swallowed up Hank Fernow after you tackled and knocked him into the water."

"You can always find a few quiet pools off the main current," Longarm said. "And a sandy beach where a man and woman can . . ."

"Damn, Custis, you sure do have some recuperative powers."

"Recuperative what?"

"Don't play dumb with me," Shotgun Sallie warned with a smile. "You know exactly what I'm talking about here."

"Then what do you say we camp by a beach on the way up to your ranch and push a little sand around together in the moonlight?"

"That is the best idea I've heard today," she told him. "Now let's quit acting foolish and get the buckboard hitched up and ready to roll. Time is wastin', Custis."

"Yeah, I know," he said. "I read somewhere that it waits for no man."

"Or woman. You visit the local marshal and your federal office?"

"I did."

"And?"

Longarm thought a moment. "The local marshal and I had a few hard words and he told me that he didn't want me to come back to Denver."

She looked closely at him. "And you said?"

"My words to Marshal Oscar Duncan aren't fit for a lady to hear," he said with a laugh in his voice.

"Well, then, you can tell me exactly what you said to the man on the way up to Central City," Shotgun Sallie told him. "Because you know that I'm *not* a lady."

"Shotgun, tonight I'll thank my lucky stars for that," Longarm told her with a wink and a lecherous grin.

Chapter 15

"This is beautiful country up here," Longarm told Shotgun Sallie as they crossed meadows and drove through towering stands of pine, aspen and alder. "How many acres do you own up here on this mountain?"

"About sixteen hundred."

"That's a nice-sized ranch."

"Custis, that's not enough to call the Shotgun Ranch a big operation, but up in this country the summer grass is deep and both cattle and horses do thrive on it. In the fall, I push most of my cattle down to low country."

"It's a good living, I'd guess."

"Not the way I run the ranch," Shotgun Sallie admitted. "I have too many horses and not enough cattle. Too many cowboys past their prime, and I take in women who wouldn't otherwise have a roof over their heads or a plate of food at a table."

"Ex-prostitutes?"

"Mostly," Shotgun said. "Quite a number of them are girls who worked at my whorehouse during my early and wilder days."

"You're a soft touch, Shotgun."

"Some people think that," she agreed. "But what is supposed to happen to these lonely working girls who fell on hard times when they lost their youth and beauty? And a cowboy will always be a cowboy, even after he's gotten busted up. I've learned that hard-nosed cattle ranchers often refuse to cut them any slack and so they fire older cowboys out of hand when they've been hurt and can't measure up to the younger hands."

"How many people live on the Shotgun Ranch?" Longarm said with mild curiosity.

"Counting you and my new man Bert?"

"Yeah."

Shotgun Sallie thought about it for a few moments as they rattled down the potholed road toward a distant ranch house set back in pines. "Well," she finally said, "I will now have eleven people living at the ranch, not including myself. And you're going to be the youngest by far."

"Hellfire, Shotgun, you haven't got a ranch. You've got a sanctuary for the old and infirm!"

"Everybody on my ranch works a little," she countered. "Bert will be expected not only to keep sober, but to earn his keep at my horse barn."

"Hear that, Bert?" Longarm called over his shoulder. "This isn't going to be all milk and honey."

"I heard it," the man lying in the back of the buckboard shouted back. "And that's the way I like things. I never got nothin' for free and I don't expect to on the Shotgun Ranch."

Longarm studied the single-level ranch house just up ahead. It was huge and rambling with wings going off in several directions. He counted at least four stone chimneys and there was a long porch all the way across the front of the house lined with rocking chairs mostly filled with a colorful group of people. Some waved, recognizing Shotgun Sallie, and some just sat and rocked with smiles on their lined faces. Even before they rolled into the ranch yard, Longarm could see that most of the men and women were in their sixties or older.

"This place looks to me like a Civil War veteran's nursing home," Longarm said.

"It isn't," Shotgun countered. "Every one of these good people is the victim of hard and unlucky circumstances. Every one of them is honest and kind. Some bear bitterness in their hearts; most all of them have aches and pains. But you'll come to know they are a nice, friendly bunch with some very interesting life stories."

"How do you support all these people?"

"I sure as hell don't from my cattle or horses," she told him. "My brothel up in Central City is very, very busy and profitable and it pays for the ranch expenses. I have an honest manager running things for me in Central City who is a longtime friend and will one day live here on the Shotgun Ranch. I ride down to Central City often and check up on things, but I don't really run the whorehouse anymore. No need to do that when there is so much that needs doing up here at Shotgun Ranch."

Longarm pulled the buckboard up before the big log house and several men all limping and looking to be far past their best years came out to help unload supplies and get Bert Hollister out of the wagon.

"Where do you want us to put this one up?" a tall, skinny man with a shock of white hair asked.

"Put him in the west wing," Shotgun Sallie said. "Bert can room with Jesse. They're both old cowboys so they should get along just fine."

"Jesse can be cantankerous and he likes his privacy," the man warned.

"Well," Shotgun Sallie mused, "if Jesse complains, tell him I said that there's a lot of room for him to camp out in my horse barn. That ought to keep him in line and of a decent frame of mind."

The man grinned. "I expect it will." He extended his hand to Longarm. "My name is Earl. Earl Boyer. I was a Texas Ranger in the early years down along the border. Fought with Sam Houston and we whipped Santa Anna's ass and made the arrogant bastard pay for what he did to the brave boys who died at the Alamo and Goliad. My only regret is that we didn't hang Santa Anna by his little balls."

Longarm nodded. "This is Bert Hollister. He likes horses better than people, but he won't bite your head off."

"If he tried to do that," Earl said, "I'd whip his ass, only it looks like someone already beat me to it."

"Yeah," Longarm said, "but Bert has a way of getting even, so don't let his sad present condition fool you. Bert is tough."

"I'll be sure to keep that in mind," Earl said. "I've worked my way up here to become the ranch carpenter and handyman. I can build a table, chairs, staircases, or damned near anything that Shotgun wants. I oversaw the building of a new wing on the ranch house two years ago and, if more of you keep coming, I'm going to form a crew of the old farts and build an east wing. Plenty of timber around here for it."

"And I'm the cook," a woman in her sixties said. "Name is Annie. I can cook the tail of a coyote and make it tasty. I can cook an old turkey vulture so tender you'd think it was grain-fed pheasant."

"Well then," Longarm said good-naturedly, "don't tell

me what you're *really* cooking when I sit down at your table and I'll be a lot happier."

"Fair enough," Annie said with a giggle as she waddled back up onto the porch and plopped down in a rocking chair.

And so the chatter went as Longarm was introduced to the men and women who lived on the Shotgun Ranch in a state of easy and congenial semiretirement. What was immediately clear to Longarm was that everyone not only got along with each other, but they adored Shotgun Sallie. There was no scraping or bending to their boss, just genuine love and respect for the madam of a very profitable whorehouse.

Longarm was given his own room and he was pleased to discover it was located right next to the one Shotgun slept in every night. If anyone thought that was indicative of his relationship with their lovely employer, they never gave the slightest indication of the fact. Longarm took a bath and that evening he took a chair beside Shotgun Sallie in a dining room almost spacious enough to have housed a locomotive.

The food came in from Annie's noisy and bustling kitchen on huge steaming platters. Ham, beef, chicken . . . or turkey vulture . . . vegetables from the ranch's own vast garden, and fresh milk and butter from three brown cows that lived out in the horse barn.

Glancing up and down the long table and hearing a half dozen conversations going at the same time with a great deal of laughter mixed in for good measure, Longarm was struck by what a happy family Shotgun Sallie had collected. But then he went and spoiled the thought by wondering what would happen here if the entire Fernow Clan

showed up looking for revenge against him and Shotgun
Sallie. Longarm figured that all these nice old folks would
be willing to put their lives on the line to save their lady
boss and fight the Fernow Clan, but if they dared to do that
they would be slaughtered like lambs before a pack of
starving wolves.

And realizing that fact, Longarm suddenly lost his appe-
tite and sense of humor.

Chapter 16

Longarm spent a full week resting and recuperating at the Shotgun Ranch, but he never really relaxed for a moment. Shotgun Sallie wanted to involve him in the ranching business and told him far more than he wanted to know about raising cattle. He did spend a good deal of those first days down at the horse barn, where Bert was obviously in his element.

"You ever seen finer horses than these?" Bert asked, gesturing toward a grassy pasture where four mares with foals grazed. "Why, if I'd have had horses that looked like these when I was a working cowboy, I'd have been cock of the walk! And they ain't just easy on the eye. Miss Shotgun Sallie told me that she is raisin' these horses for what she calls 'performance.'"

"Which means?" Longarm asked.

"Which means they are so fast and quick that they can work cattle even in heavy timber and brush country. Why, these are the kind of horses that can turn on a biscuit and never even break the crust. Custis, I swear that there ain't a jug head on the ranch, and every one of 'em can run and rein so quick they'd throw dirt in the eyes of a jumpin' jackrabbit. I've just never seen anything to match this bunch of Shotgun Ranch horses."

Longarm grinned and he was immensely pleased to see the enthusiasm that Bert was feeling. "You think they're pretty special, huh?"

"Not only special, but every one of these Shotgun horses is worth a whole lot of money. See those four mares and foals? Why, I've met ranchers that would give a thousand dollars for every pair and think that they stole 'em."

Custis tipped back his flat-brimmed Stetson. "Shotgun Sallie told me that the cattle are just for eatin' grass, but these horses are something very special to her."

"They ought to be," Bert said. "She's got a stallion in the far pasture that is the finest horse I've ever laid eyes upon. He's a chestnut and so handsome an animal that he ought to be ashamed of himself. Miss Sallie told me that he was a Morgan, but I don't know what that means."

"I've heard of them," Longarm said. "And I remember seeing quite a few back in West Virginia where I was born and raised. They're highly prized animals. Morgan horses are not real big, but they're almost always strong, fast, and sure-footed."

"Well, this chestnut-colored stallion fits that description. I asked Jesse if the stallion was mannerly and he said you could put a child on his back as long as the kid didn't wear spurs. He said that Miss Sallie won five hundred dollars racing the stallion in Central City. Seems there was a bay horse that was called a Thoroughbred and that nothing could match for speed. Well, Miss Sallie got on that chestnut stallion and when the race was over she was so far in the lead folks said that it looked like a hog chasin' an antelope."

Longarm laughed out loud. "I find that a little hard to believe, Bert. But it doesn't matter. Just looking at those mares and their foals, anyone could tell that they were sired by an exceptional horse."

Bert surveyed the mountain peaks ringing the ranch and sighed. "This ranch sure is the prettiest spread I ever worked on."

"How are you doing without the whiskey?"

"So far, so good," Bert told him. "The first few days here were the roughest, but I was in such terrible shape from the beating that I didn't notice the shakes as much as I did later. Now I'm starting to feel pretty good. Sorry, sure. But I'm gonna make it up here, Marshal. I've made up my mind that I've had my last drink and from now on I'm gonna stay as sober as a preacher on Sunday."

"I've seen some preachers that get drunk every Sunday night," Longarm said. "So be careful."

"Aw," Bert told him. "Where am I gonna get a drink even if I wanted one? Which I don't."

"A drunk can always find a drink," Longarm cautioned. "So you just keep that in mind when the day comes that you have your chance to go to town and see the elephant dance."

"I will. But the truth is that those last years in Denver I just plumb wore myself out bendin' my elbow to look up the neck of a bottle. And by and by the liquor worked its way clear down to the heels of my boots and ate 'em off."

"I expect that it did," Longarm said. "Think I'll take a walk and get some exercise. I've been lying around and I'm getting restless."

"I'd keep you company except I'm still a little under the weather, so to speak."

"I'll be fine, Bert."

"You might want to take your rifle, Marshal. Could be you'll come across a nice fat buck for the table."

Longarm studied the old cowboy. "You're not really thinking of deer or elk right now, are you?"

"No," Bert admitted. "I was thinking of the Fernow boys."

"You believe they might be coming here?"

"Of course they will. By now we've been gone from Denver for more than a week and they'll be missing Otis and Hank. Could be they've already gone and found out that one of 'em is buried and that you are the one that shot him . . . even though I really did it."

Longarm nodded in agreement. "Maybe you have a point, Bert. I'll get my Winchester before I take that hike."

"Figure you ought to do that," Bert said, looking relieved. "Because the way I'm thinkin', it's not a matter of *if*, it's just a matter of *when* those bloody bastards find out we're here. And when they do, hell will be a-poppin'."

"Might be better if I went and talked to them before it comes to that," Longarm mused.

"You ride off to do that, it will only mean the best man on this ranch will be pushin' up daisies and of no earthly good to the rest of us when the Fernow men come for Miss Sallie. Don't forget that they know she blew off Melvin Fernow's damned head up in your room."

"I haven't forgotten anything, Bert."

"Then don't go too far away, and keep your powder dry and your eyes sharp," the old cowboy warned. "Because I got a feelin' them Fernow bastards are a-gatherin' someplace not far away, and like a terrible black storm, they are comin' to rain down on all of us."

"You're a real cloud of gloom today," Longarm said.

"Gloom hell!" Bert snapped. "I just believe that they're comin' and it won't be long before all hell breaks loose here. You thought about how all these old folks are gonna handle it when the Fernow men come for the three of us?"

"I've thought about it," Longarm replied.

"Well, think harder then," Bert snapped. "And come up with some way that we can get through this trouble alive."

"I will, Bert. I surely will do that," Longarm promised as he walked back toward the ranch house.

Chapter 17

Longarm went back to his room and retrieved his Winchester while also strapping his revolver and gun belt to his hip. Early that morning Shotgun Sallie had ridden into nearby Central City to see how things were going at her whorehouse. As the day had worn on, Longarm began to regret that he had not accompanied Shotgun Sallie.

What if the Fernow Clan had already rallied forces and was even now in Central City?

When Longarm thought about that clan of killers he wondered if he should go find them before they attacked him and Shotgun Sallie. Maybe whoever had replaced Kenyon Fernow as clan leader was more intelligent and reasonable than Kenyon had been. Perhaps he would be willing to listen to Longarm and agree to peace.

But Longarm knew that wasn't likely. And the other thing he had to remind himself of was that he had not yet fully recovered from his wounds and injuries, which would reduce his chances of surviving a gunfight. However, the idea of them coming to this beautiful ranch populated by older people and imposing their vengeance and brutality was entirely unacceptable.

So what should he do? This was the question that was plaguing his mind as he strolled out toward the pines that ringed the pastures and hay fields of the Shotgun Ranch.

Fifteen minutes after leaving the ranch house, Longarm was beside a fence post watching Shotgun Sallie's prized chestnut stallion graze in the sweet mountain grass. The sun was gliding down toward the western peaks and there were big white clouds on the eastern horizon that promised rain.

Suddenly, the stallion spooked and whirled. The magnificent animal threw its head up and its nostrils dilated as it sniffed the wind and stared into the pine trees. The horse snorted and pranced around in a tight, nervous circle, eyes locked on a place where the forest was thickest.

Longarm's own eyes tracked those of the stallion as he searched for the cause of its sudden alarm. Had the chestnut seen an elk or a buck that Longarm could shoot with his Winchester?

When the stallion's agitation increased and it began to whinny, Longarm felt himself tense with suspicion. The chestnut would not have become so agitated by an elk or a buck, and that meant whatever had caught and held the animal's attention was definitely not wild game.

And then, like a bolt of lightning, he had his answer . . . the Fernow men!

The realization struck Longarm precisely the same instant his eye caught movement and the glint of gunmetal.

"Damn!" Longarm swore, diving to the ground as the cedar fence post next to him splintered under the impact of a rifle shell. "Damn!"

Longarm was out in an open pasture, but the pasture grass was about two feet high, so he stayed pinned to the ground, listening as Shotgun Sallie's chestnut stallion galloped toward the horse barn. Two more rifle shots split the air overhead like thunder and Longarm got his rifle into position and tried to peer through the tall grass in order to find a target.

His heart was hammering as he patiently waited while probing bullets were unleashed in his direction. It was obvious that the rifleman or riflemen hiding in the pine forest had no idea of his exact position.

Longarm heard shouts from the ranch house and twisted around to see Bert and Jesse coming toward him with pistols in their hands.

"Get back to the ranch house!" Longarm shouted, knowing that the two former cowboys would be easy pickings and had no hope of putting up a good fight armed only with revolvers. "Bert! Jesse! I'm all right! Go back!"

But Bert had no intention of going anywhere except to Longarm's aid. The old cowboy kept coming, limping and struggling, while his roommate, Jesse, stopped in his tracks, looking as if he was unsure of what to do before turning and heading back toward the house.

"Bert, go back!" Longarm shouted frantically.

His shouted warning only seemed to make Bert Hollister try harder to reach his side. The cowboy was less than fifty feet away when a rifle slug cut him down. Longarm jumped to his feet and ran, diving to the man's side in a hail of bullets.

"Bert!"

"Git them bastards!" Bert hissed. "Kill 'em to the very last . . . man!"

Longarm tore open the man's shirt and saw that his wound was bleeding fast but that it wasn't fatal. "Dammit, Bert! You should have stayed at the ranch house and grabbed a rifle."

"Well there wasn't time!" Bert argued. "How bad am I shot?"

"It's just a flesh wound," Longarm told him. "Press your hand down on the wound and try to keep from losing so much blood."

"What are you going to do?" Bert asked through clenched teeth.

"Try to stay alive," Longarm replied. "And maybe pick off a few more of the Fernow men."

"It sure didn't take 'em long to come for us," Bert growled. "I figured them for another week or two."

"We've killed a lot of them and I'm sure they're crazy for revenge," Longarm told the wounded cowboy. "Now, Bert, stay down and stay still and quiet. I'm going to roll off a ways and see if I can't do some damage with this Winchester."

"If they put one in you, be sure and holler, Marshal. That way I'll know they're comin' to finish me off as well and I'll make 'em pay with this six-gun. By damn, I'll get one or two more before they get me!"

"All right," Longarm promised. "If I get hit badly, I'll holler. Until then, promise me you'll stay low and quiet."

"Okay," Bert said, blood leaking through his thick fingers. "I sure wish I had a bottle of whiskey right now. Medicinal, of course."

"Of course," Longarm said with a tight grin as he rolled over and over, wanting to move away from the wounded man.

Longarm could hear the Fernow men shouting in the pines. He reckoned they were arguing over his state of health and trying to decide if they should move out of the pines and close in for the kill . . . or if that might get some of them killed.

*Come on out, boys! I'm waiting for you in the tall grass.
Try to find me while I cut you down.*

These were Longarm's grim thoughts as he removed his
six-gun from his holster and laid it out beside the rifle. Both
weapons were loaded, and he knew that no matter how
many Fernow men came to finish him off, he would be able
to sell his life very dearly.

Longarm was in a killing frame of mind as lifted his body
an inch or two off the grass and waited for a target. He didn't
have to wait long until one of the ambushers showed himself.
Longarm took a very quick aim and squeezed his trigger less
than two heartbeats later.

"Ahhh!"

A high-pitched and terrible scream, immediately followed by the sound of wild thrashing, told Longarm in
grim and unmistakable terms that he'd found and either
badly wounded or killed his first target. Longarm rolled
twice and hunkered tight against the pasture floor, knowing
what would happen next.

Like an overturned hornet's nest, a hail of bullets came
flying his way. But Longarm waited out the volley, and
when the rifles silenced, he could hear someone screaming
in pain and another in fury.

"You bastard, you gut-shot Billy!" a Fernow bellowed,
losing his mind in rage and charging out of the trees.

"Join him in hell," Longarm whispered as he again took
aim and shot the ambusher who howled and struggled to
rise from his knees. Longarm drew a steady bead on the
wounded man and drilled him through the heart with his
next bullet.

He flattened on the grass as another hail of bullets
passed overhead. Moments passed and the silence deep-
ened as the sun touched the crest of the Rockies. Longarm

knew that it would be dark within a half hour, and then what would happen? Would they try to encircle the Shotgun Ranch house and lay siege? With enough food and ammunition, they could ring the ranch house for days . . . even weeks.

"Fernow!" Longarm yelled. "This is Marshal Custis Long from Denver, and you sonsabitches better throw down your weapons and come out with your hands up. You're *all* under arrest!"

A ragged, deep voice came back at him. "You want us, come and find us, Marshal! And when you do, you can pick up what's left of the woman!"

When Longarm heard those words his heart almost froze in his chest.

Did they have Shotgun Sallie? Had they already murdered her? Or was this just a clever or desperate bluff?

There was really only one way to answer that question, and that was to hold tight until the sun went down and get Bert back to the ranch house. After that Longarm would go manhunting with the full intention of doing exactly what poor Bert Hollister had urged him to do.

Git them bastards! Kill 'em to the very last man.

Chapter 18

It had seemed to take forever before the sun went down. Once darkness had fallen over the pasture, Longarm hurried over to Bert and whispered, "How you holding up, cowboy?"

"I need a drink of whiskey in the worst possible way or I'm not gonna make it, Marshal."

"You'll drink nothing but milk or water when I get you back to the ranch house," Longarm promised. He looked out toward the ranch house and yelled, "Hey, Jesse!"

"Yeah?"

"I'm bringing Bert in so don't shoot us in the dark!"

"I'm with everyone else in the ranch house!" Jesse hollered. "Everyone in here is armed to the teeth."

"Don't let them get trigger happy when we cross the yard."

"What about them gawdamn Fernow men?"

"I don't know," Longarm answered. "Here we come."

He grabbed Bert and pulled him to his feet and half carried, half dragged the wounded cowboy up to the ranch house.

"My gawd, he's been shot!" an old ex-prostitute named Rose cried as she hurried to assist the barely conscious Bert. "We can't lay him on Miss Sallie's new sofa or it'll be ruined and she'll be furious."

"Lay me on the damned floor," Bert snapped, more awake than he'd seemed. "And get me some of her good *whiskey*!"

"Get him a glass of water, and I'll need plenty of bandaging," Longarm told the ring of old people standing around Bert in fear and confusion. "Hurry up!"

Bert protested, saying, "Hell, I'm gonna die for certain if I don't get a drink of whiskey, so if all you're gonna give me is water then you might just as well let me croak, then stand at the Pearly Gates."

"Shut up," Longarm told the grouchy old drunk. "You're sober and that's the way you're staying."

Twenty minutes later, Bert was bandaged up and lying on his own bed, snoring. Longarm moved back into the big living room and looked at all the lined and worried faces.

"I know that you're all concerned about what happened out there in the south pasture," he began, choosing his words carefully. "It was the Fernow men doing most of the shooting after they almost ambushed me. They'd have succeeded, too, if the chestnut stallion hadn't alerted me a split second before they opened fire. Then Bert and Jesse came running, and Bert was wounded."

Longarm turned to look at the other cowboy staying at the ranch. "Jesse, are you all right?"

"I'm as happy as a fly on a fresh turd," the old cowboy said. "But I'm mad enough to eat the Devil with his horns on, and I sure wish that I'd have shot one or two of them bastards like you did, Marshal."

"Jesse, did you hear one of the Fernow men shout that they have Shotgun Sallie?"

"Can't say that I did. You see, my hearin' ain't so good anymore. And my old ticker was poundin' so loud in my ears that I didn't hear much of anything except rifle fire."

Longarm took a deep breath. He placed his hands on his hips and surveyed the collection of people standing around waiting for him to take command of the situation. "Folks, here's the bad news. One of the Fernow men hiding in the pines shouted that they had captured a woman, and there isn't much doubt that he was referring to Shotgun Sallie."

"How'd they do that?" a small but still attractive woman asked. "That woman would never surrender to anyone. They'd have had to kill Miss Sallie before she let them lay their filthy hands on her."

"I don't know the answer to your question," Longarm admitted. "All I know for sure is that she was supposed to leave her business in Central City and return to this ranch before dark."

"Well, we can't all just sit around here and wait to see if she's okay or not," Jesse said. "I'm going to saddle a horse right now and go lookin' for her."

"Now hold on there," Longarm cautioned. "Let's think this out for a few minutes before we jump the gun and do something stupid. We have to remember, the Fernow men are vicious and cunning. They'd probably like all of us men to saddle up and go racing off to the rescue toward Central City. Then they'd be able to walk into this place and do whatever they wanted to the ladies . . . and Bert. As vengeful as they are, I wouldn't put it past them to kill every one of you women and then burn this house to the ground. Is that what anyone here wants?"

They all shook their heads, even more upset and confused than they'd been moments earlier.

"So what can we do?" Rose demanded.

"I'll ride to Central City alone. Jesse, you and the men are going to have to stand guard all night and until I return. Bring the chestnut stallion and the mares and their foals into the barn and post a few people there to watch over them so that nobody comes and torches the barn. Others of you will need to stay here and guard this house from attack."

They exchanged glances, nodding, so Longarm continued. "I'll leave here right away and I should be in Central City long before midnight. I'll go to Shotgun's whorehouse first and make sure she was there checking up on things earlier in the day. Maybe she's *still* there."

"Now why on earth would she still be there?" an older prostitute named Rabbit—because of her buck teeth—wanted to know.

"Rabbit, I have no idea."

"Well, if you're thinking she stayed to make a few extra dollars herself, forget that idea!"

"It never entered my mind that she'd get on a mattress today. But maybe she suddenly fell ill or had a problem with one of the girls or a customer. Many things could have gone wrong during Shotgun Sallie's visit and made it necessary for her to stay over for the night. I just have to find out if she's there or not."

"You ever even been to her place?" Rabbit demanded.

"Can't say that I have," Longarm answered.

"Do you know how to find it?"

"Nope."

"It's called the Hairy Hole Hotel and it's about a quarter of a mile this side of town on the right side of the road. Big, two-story brick building with a porch and a red lantern hanging for anyone to see at any time of night."

"That's the damnedest name I ever heard of for a whorehouse," Longarm said, shaking his head.

"Well, that's what she renamed it just out of spite when the church women tried get her run out of Central City. Before that it was named—"

"Never mind," Longarm interrupted. "I'll find it, all right."

"They might be tucked away up in the Hairy Hole waiting to ambush you when you walk in the door," Milly offered.

"You're right," Longarm said, nodding. "So is there a back door?"

"Sure, it opens up to face three handsome red, white, and blue shitters standing side by side about twenty feet behind the building. Those shitters each have a red lantern hanging on their fronts to guide the night customers as well as the girls."

"Them shitters are the nicest I ever used," Rabbit said, nodding her head with conviction. "Miss Sallie keeps a Chinaman on the payroll and he cleans 'em every single morning with soap and hot water. I don't know how Chen Lee stands it, but he does. He has this wooden bucket and he scoops—"

"Never mind about the Chinaman," Longarm said, cutting her off before she could give him the disgusting details.

"You're going to bring Miss Sallie back to us safe and sound, ain't you?"

"If she's alive, I'll find and bring her back," Longarm vowed. "If she's already dead . . . well, God have mercy on the Fernow men because I won't."

"If she's dead, you gotta come back for us," Jesse stated. "We're going to want to have our due and not just let you do all the killin'."

"Let's just hope that she's all right. Meantime, Jesse, I'm leaving you in charge of setting up the guards for the horse barn and this house. Take turns and keep awake and listen sharp."

"Most of us are half deaf," Milly admitted. "But we'll be all right until you and Miss Sallie come back."

"Good. I'm leaving."

"If you aren't back by daybreak," Jesse said, "I'm saddling a horse and coming to town."

"All right," Longarm replied, knowing he wasn't going to change the old cowboy's mind. "But until then, be alert for anything."

"We will," Rabbit said.

"And check on Bert to make sure that he doesn't start bleeding again. And whatever you do, don't let him talk you into a glass or two of whiskey."

"Not a chance of that," Jesse promised.

"Good. Those of you who pray, offer a few words for your boss and friend."

"And what are those of us who don't pray to do?" Rabbit asked.

"Just . . . just be ready to fight if I go down out there and Miss Sallie is already dead, because the Fernow men are vengeful and ruthless. If they're like Kenyon Fernow, the patriarch of the family who I killed years ago near Granite Creek, then they'll want every last one of you dead and this place burned to the ground before their bloodlust is slaked."

"We women here ain't shrinkin' violets that don't know how to protect ourselves," Rabbit told him. "We've all had to use a knife or a gun somewhere along the line in our profession to stay alive. So even if you and Miss Sallie are gone, we'll make damn good and sure that the Fernow Clan reaps what it sows."

Longarm studied the faces of the former prostitutes, and a world of misery but also steel and determination was to be seen in the lines of their faces, the flinty look in their eyes and the collective set of their jaws.

"I know that you won't go down easily," he said. "And when I find the Fernow men that tried to kill me, I'll rest easier for knowing you will survive even if I don't."

There being nothing more to say, Longarm went into his room and retrieved an extra pistol, which he stuck under his cartridge belt. Then, with his Winchester in hand, he strode out the front door, leaving Shotgun Sallie's collection of elderly and damaged friends.

Chapter 19

Longarm rode grimly along in the moonlight with his mind set on only one thing, and that was to find Shotgun Sallie alive and then somehow get her safely away from the Fernow men. He had chosen to ride an elegant bay gelding that Jesse said was fast, sure-footed, and sensible to ride.

The road that connected the Shotgun Ranch with Central City followed the course of a shallow mountain stream that was now sparkling like diamonds in the Rocky Mountain moonlight. There was just enough light to see silhouettes of trees, rocks, and buildings and although Longarm was anxious about Shotgun Sallie's welfare, he did not hurry, preferring to move the bay along at a steady, purposeful jog.

About two miles from Central City he began to observe more farms and buildings, some occupied and some deserted. He heard dogs barking and now and then voices that carried clearly in the thin, cool night air.

Once, Longarm heard a distant gunshot. Just one, and it faintly echoed into silence.

As he grew closer to Central City, Longarm pushed the Shotgun Ranch Morgan into an easy canter. Every fiber of his body was strung tight and he leaned forward in the saddle, eyes probing the darkness, ears alert for any more gunshots or other sounds. But none were heard and so he continued to canter the Morgan at a collected pace until he entered the outskirts of the mining town and then he reined his horse to a standstill and listened hard.

He detected no unusual sounds, no cries of distress or even the anxious barking of dogs that were upset or alarmed. Nothing told him that trouble was just a short way ahead.

"I hope she's still at the Hairy Hole Hotel," Longarm said aloud to himself. "And that Shotgun Sallie has just decided to stay over for the night because of some unforeseen business or personal problem involving one of her girls."

But then as he was passing an abandoned blacksmith shop several minutes later, Longarm saw the looming silhouettes of at least eight or ten riders coming toward him from town. They sounded loud, drunk, and boisterous. Longarm knew that these men could be cowboys leaving town after an evening of drinking and whoring, but an inner warning told him that they were his enemies—the Fernow men.

He abruptly reined the bay gelding hard off the road and trotted around behind the abandoned blacksmith shop, hoping that he had not been spotted by the approaching riders. The bay was nervous and stomping around but it didn't whinny.

"Easy," Longarm crooned to the animal. "Easy."

When the gelding calmed a little, Longarm used his reins to tie it securely to a tree back in the shadows. He yanked his Winchester out of his saddle scabbard and moved at a running crouch toward the road where he then knelt behind cover as the group of horsemen drew abreast of his hiding place.

"This is going to be good," a rider crowed, his voice slurred from whiskey. "We'll catch 'em all in one house and we'll burn it to the ground."

"I hear there's some whores livin' at the Shotgun Ranch," another drunken voice said. "Even after the ones we just had for free at the Hairy Hole, I still ain't satisfied. I'm ready for more women!"

One of them hiccupped. "You fools, we all know that the ones at the ranch are *old* whores. Old and *ugly*."

"Yeah, maybe so, but whores are still whores," the first man said, giggling drunkenly. "I say we take some pleasure before we torch the house."

"Me, too," someone agreed. "But we gotta remember that Marshal Long is hiding among them whores and old used-up bastards. *He's* the one we gotta kill first."

"Why don't you all shut your traps!" a man sounding a lot more sober than his companions snarled.

"Who's got a bottle?"

"I do," came the answer, "but you drunk yours and this one's all mine."

"Gimme that bottle!"

There was some arguing and Longarm heard a rider's body hit the road after he fell off his horse.

"Get him the hell back in his saddle!" the sober one ordered. "And stop messing around! We got killing to do and you'd better be able to handle it right."

"I can handle anything. But Howard is so drunk he can't hardly stick to this saddle and can't ride no more."

"By gawd, he'll climb back in his saddle and ride or I'll get down and kick his ass up between his shoulder blades!

And as for the Denver marshal, he'll either come out of the house unarmed or we'll shoot the woman in her ranch yard and then we'll torch her house."

Hearing this, Longarm knew that Shotgun Sallie was still alive and right now she was riding past him, bound and gagged. He listened to more of the drunken and scattered talk as the Fernow men passed him going up the road before he hurried back and untied the bay Morgan.

What was he going to do now to get Shotgun Sallie out of their clutches?

Longarm could only think of one answer, and that was to reach the Shotgun Ranch before this drunken clan and sound a warning to his waiting friends.

He untied the bay gelding, shoved his rifle into his saddle scabbard, and mounted the animal. Because the wagon road that the Fernow men were traveling was in a canyon, there wasn't a lot of room to outflank this bunch. That being the case, Longarm figured he had no choice but to ride directly into the stream and try to force the gelding to move fast enough through the shallow water until he was past the Fernow men. After that he could get back onto the road and try to put some distance between himself and the heavily armed and vengeance-minded Fernow Clan.

His plan worked well. The Morgan wasn't real happy about going into the stream but once it was out in the middle of the water it trotted obligingly and never once lost its slippery underwater footing.

"Come on, boy," Longarm whispered, standing in his stirrups and forcing the Morgan to move faster. The splash of his horse's hooves was loud but Longarm was hoping that the drunken Fernow men had continued to talk and argue so that their voices would mask his streambed passing.

Longarm pushed the Morgan hard, and when he was

certain that he had to be well upstream from the clan, he urged his bay horse out of the water and back onto the dirt road. He'd be leaving fresh tracks and maybe even wet ones, but would the Fernow men, so sure of their murderous plan and confident in their number, even notice?

Time and distance were running out on him, so Longarm forced the Morgan into a full gallop. He went charging up the road and onto the ranch property. Up ahead he could see that Jesse had ordered almost all the ranch lamps to be extinguished.

Longarm knew that he was running a real risk of being shot out of his saddle by Jesse and the others hiding both inside the barn and the ranch house. So as he drew to within a hundred yards of the house, he shouted, "It's me! Marshal Custis Long! Nobody shoot!"

A moment later, the dark forms of men and women came pouring out of the ranch house and barn.

"What the hell you doin'!" Jesse demanded with a rifle in his fists. "Where's Miss Sallie!"

Longarm jumped off his horse and, with the crowd pressing around him, he explained the circumstances, ending with, "There are eight or ten riders and one of them is Shotgun Sallie. We've got to figure out a way to get her away from the Fernow men or they'll kill her for certain."

"She'll probably be the shortest rider and . . ."

"She might *not* be the shortest," Longarm argued.

"We can recognize her by her *horse*," Jesse said, his voice now filled with excitement. "This morning early I saddled up a nice buckskin mare so she could ride it into Central City. Ain't likely that there will be *two* buckskins in the bunch coming here."

Longarm's mind was racing. "You're right, Jesse. What else can we look for so she doesn't get shot by mistake?"

"She was wearing dangling gold earrings," Rabbit offered. "They might gleam in this moonlight."

"Sure, they might!" Jesse said. "But those Fernow men are probably going to keep Miss Sallie right in the middle of their pack. So how the hell are we going to shoot them without shooting her instead?"

Everyone seemed to turn to Longarm for the answer, and for a moment, he didn't have a clue as to how to separate Shotgun Sallie from the Fernow men without getting her killed in what was going to be a deadly cross fire.

"Spook all the horses," Bert said, limping out onto the porch and hanging weakly to a post. "Do something so spooky and bad that every horse they got will go crazy right in this ranch yard."

"Great idea!" Longarm said. "Bert, what will do that?"

Bert sagged and thought a minute before he said, "I reckon a stick of dynamite would do the job right well."

"Yeah," Jesse snapped, "but it would also kill all of 'em, including Miss Sallie!"

From the back of the group Milly threw up her small hand and offered, "Shotgun Sallie always shoots off strings of Chinese firecrackers on the Fourth of July. This year she didn't use them all and I know the drawer where she keeps the ones left over for next year."

"Get them for me!" Longarm ordered, urgency high in his voice. "Milly, hurry!"

While Milly rushed back into the house for the string of firecrackers, Longarm laid out a quick but what he hoped would be an effective plan.

"Jesse, you and a couple of others go back into the house and that will draw the Fernow men into the yard. Let them see one of you sitting in the window reading something like you don't have a worry in the world."

"But I can't read," Jesse replied with a pained expression.

"It doesn't matter. Just *look* like you're reading."

"Why?"

"When the Fernow men ride into this yard it has to appear that no one at the house is expecting trouble. We are going to need to hit them before they realize they're caught in a trap."

Longarm surveyed the other household members. "Those of you who are armed can go circle the ranch yard and stay hidden. I'll hide in the horse barn with the firecrackers, and when the Fernow men are between me and the ranch house, I'll light the firecrackers and sneak in behind the riders. If I'm lucky and quiet, I'll get close enough to toss the string of firecrackers under the legs of their horses."

"But Miss Sallie will go up with all the rest of 'em!" someone protested. "She could end up getting thrown and trampled to death."

"I know," Longarm said. "But that's the only hope we have of getting her away from them alive."

Longarm waited until all of them were hanging on his next words and then said, "When the firecrackers go off and all hell is breaking loose, men and horses will be flying in every direction. I'll be in the middle of that mess trying to pick Shotgun Sallie out so that I can drag her into the barn and away from danger. So whatever you people do, stay well hidden until I yell that I've got her safe in the barn, and then open up on the Fernow men with everything you've got. Is that clear?"

They nodded, weapons clenched tight in their old fists.

"Okay," Longarm said, taking their measure and believing they were up to this bloody work, "now everyone hide around the yard. No matter what, don't let them know they're riding into a trap. Because if one of you sneezes, coughs, or even farts, those Fernow men will bolt and ride away, taking Shotgun Sallie to her death. Is this understood?"

They nodded and Longarm said, "Good. Where the hell is Milly with those Chinese firecrackers!"

"I got 'em, Marshal!"

Milly bolted off the front porch and ran to the group, out of breath. She managed to say, "Marshal, do you have matches?"

"I sure do," Longarm answered. "Milly, are you up for a gunfight?"

"Hell, yes!" She waved a derringer at him and Longarm quickly pushed it out of his face.

"Then go hide with the others. They'll tell you our plan. Now move!"

"I'm about moved out already," Milly said, gasping for breath as Longarm took the firecrackers from her and rushed toward the barn.

He didn't get into the horse barn a moment too soon. Crouched by the big barn door he heard the riders coming up to the ranch house. Heard their now-muted voices and the clink of a tossed whiskey bottle bouncing on the hard ground.

Longarm found a match and selected the last of those excellent Cuban cigars that he'd taken from Billy Vail's office. Shielded by the barn door, he lit the cigar, extinguished the match, and smoked quietly as the knot of horsemen drew up in front of the ranch house.

"Hello in there!" one of the riders shouted. "You by the window readin'. We got Shotgun Sallie, and unless you get that Denver marshal out here in about one minute, I'll put a bullet through her pretty head!"

Longarm peered around the corner of the barn door and recognized Jesse when he opened the front door and stood framed in lamplight.

"Who are you?" the old cowboy asked, actually managing to look more startled than afraid.

"Never mind who we are, you sonofabitch! Where's that Denver marshal?"

Longarm figured it was about time to move. The wick that fed the Chinese firecrackers was about a foot long and he had no idea how long it might take for that to burn and cause a string of violent explosions. But Longarm wasn't taking any chances that it would blow up in his hand, so he used the glowing tip of his cigar to light the fuse and then he crouched and tiptoed out of the barn toward the unsuspecting riders. One of them was astride a buckskin and he focused on that person.

The fuse hissed softly like a rattlesnake and when Longarm tore his eyes away from the rider on the buckskin he was shocked to see that the fuse was almost gone!

Holy shit! It's about to explode!

Using a hard sidearm motion, Longarm hurled the string of firecrackers at the rear legs of the Fernow horses. Threw it low and hard and then he recoiled as the entire string began to ignite with tremendous booms and a series of bright, crackling flashes.

All of the horses went insane! Some dropped their heads and began to buck as if their tails were on fire. One lost its mind and ran straight at the house with its rider screaming. The animal vaulted over the porch and crashed through Shotgun Sallie's big front glass window. Another flipped belly up into the sky and fell over backward, crushing its rider.

But the buckskin that Shotgun Sallie was astride went

straight up, its forelegs clawing for the moon, and when it landed Longarm was amazed to see that Shotgun Sallie was still in her saddle. With the string of firecrackers booming like the blasts of small cannon, her buckskin fishtailed as it went bucking through the ranch's vegetable garden.

The buckskin crashed headlong into a tool and garden shed, launching Shotgun Sallie into the sky.

Longarm drew his six-gun and began shooting at the Fernow men. All around the ranch yard other guns barked, muzzle flashes winking like dancing fireflies. Suddenly Longarm heard hammers clicking on empty cylinders "Hold your fire!" he shouted.

The last time he'd seen Shotgun Sallie she had just been launched by her bucking buckskin over the toolshed, and so that's where Longarm ran.

"Shotgun!" he called.

"Up here." Her voice was weak and shaky.

Longarm looked all around. "Up *where*?"

"*Here*, gawdammit!"

Longarm craned his neck toward the shed's roof to see a pair of shapely bare legs wagging at the moon. Then his eyes really popped when he saw her bare butt cheeks. Shotgun Sallie, he suddenly remembered, didn't like wearing underclothing.

"Holy cow, what a sight!" he whispered to himself a moment before he tore open the door of the shed and gazed up to see the top part of Shotgun Sallie sticking through the hole she'd punctured in the shed's roof. On her way through the roof she had torn off her blouse, and her breasts were now hanging directly overhead like big white melons.

For a moment they just stared at each other in shocked amazement but it was Shotgun Sallie who first recovered her voice. "Custis, don't just stand there gaping at me! Get me out of here!"

"I'm going to need a ladder and a little help," he managed to reply. "Be right back."

Shotgun Sallie was cussing up a storm as Longarm trotted across the yard. "Anybody know where I can find a ladder?" he asked.

Almost all of them did know. And ignoring all their anxious questioning, Longarm carried the ladder across a yard strewn with dead Fernow men. "I could use a lantern, too," he called back over his shoulder.

"No lantern!" Shotgun Sallie cried. "Custis, dammit, do you really think I want everybody to see me like *this*!"

"You are in quite a bad predicament," he said, entering the shed. "It's not going to be easy to get you out of that roof without any help."

"Well, for crissakes, do your very best, Custis! My big tits are hanging in the wind just like my bare ass!"

Longarm bit his tongue and began the tedious job of extracting an embarrassed Shotgun Sallie from the shed's flimsy shake roof. When that was accomplished, he gave her his coat and said, "Did we get all the Fernow men?"

"I wish we had," Shotgun Sallie replied. "But five of the gang stayed at my whorehouse."

Longarm nearly staggered. "What!"

"You heard me. They've got my three best girls and they were taking them off someplace when this bunch tied me up and put me in the saddle."

"But why!"

"They took 'em for pleasure but they also said they were taking them for insurance."

Longarm scowled as his eyes swept the ranch yard and counted the dead Fernow men. "Insurance against *what*?"

"Something going wrong just like this," Shotgun Sallie answered. "They said that if there were any problems here, they'd kill those girls. Custis, I wish to high heaven that we were finished with that damned Fernow Clan, but we aren't."

"No," Longarm agreed, his voice grim with determination, "and we never will be until we've killed every last Fernow man standing."

"Hey!" Rabbit yelled. "One of these Fernow bastards is still alive over here!"

Everyone hurried over to Rabbit, who was standing beside a badly wounded man lying in the dirt. Longarm knelt down and said, "Who are you?"

"Elmer Fernow," the man grunted.

"Someone bring a lantern over here!" Longarm called.

A few minutes later, they were all around the wounded man, who appeared to be quite young, possibly not even out of his teens. "Hold that lantern steady," Longarm said, carefully removing the man's blood-soaked hat and shirt.

"Am . . . am I goin' to die?" Elmer Fernow whispered. "I'm awful young to die."

"You'll die if I have anything to say about it," Jesse growled, cocking back the hammer of his pistol.

"No," Longarm ordered. "Put the gun away, Jesse."

The old cowboy angrily jammed his gun into his holster.

Longarm looked up at Shotgun Sallie. "He's bleeding pretty badly. We need to get him inside and bandaged up."

"Not before he tells us where his clansmen have taken my girls. Make him tell us."

Longarm leaned a little closer to the young man. "Where did those five men take Shotgun Sallie's whores?"

"Can't . . ."

Longarm gripped the man's arm and squeezed it hard.

"You're going to bleed to death right here if you don't tell us. Those three women didn't deserve to be taken. Now tell us or we'll walk away and leave you to die in this dirt."

The man's eyelids fluttered and Longarm was afraid that he was going to become unconscious. But Elmer rallied and whispered, "If you bandage me, I'll tell you. Otherwise, I'm prepared to die."

"All right," Shotgun Sallie allowed. "Let's get him into the house and bandage him up."

"It might be too late for that," Longarm said, noting Elmer's bone-white skin and the amount of blood he was losing.

"If it is, we'll still find my girls," she replied. "But if he will tell us, it'll make things a lot easier."

Elmer Fernow had been listening to this conversation. "If I tell you where they are, then you gotta protect me from my family or they'll kill me for damn certain."

"Not if they're *all* dead," Longarm told the bleeding man. "And that's about the only way we're going to put an end to this bloody revenge business."

Fernow nodded. "I didn't have any stake in it. My uncle, Wolf Fernow, is the one who forced us into exacting revenge."

"Is Wolf Fernow one of the five who took my whores?" Shotgun Sallie demanded.

"He is," Elmer said. "And he'll kill all of 'em, too."

"Let's get him inside, plug up his wounds, and see what he has to say," Longarm said, slipping his hands under the bleeding man's shoulders. "If we don't do it right now, he's going to bleed out for certain."

Shotgun Sallie nodded, and a moment later they were carrying young Fernow into her ranch house.

Chapter 20

"Wake him up!" Shotgun Sallie ordered when the bandaging was finished. "My girls are in danger and this is no time for him to be getting his damned beauty rest."

Longarm tried to rouse Elmer Fernow, but the kid had lost so much blood he didn't seem to want to come around. Finally, Shotgun Sallie slapped Elmer hard across the face, twice, and the young man's eyes fluttered open.

"You're bandaged and we're going to try to save your worthless hide," Sallie told Elmer. "But you have to help us find my girls or I'll personally put the last bullet in your carcass." To emphasize her point, she raised a gun and cocked it over the man's face.

Elmer swallowed hard. "How many bullets did I already take?"

"Three," Longarm told him. "One grazed your skull and took off part of your ear. Another hit you in the arm, and the last one passed through your leg."

Elmer clenched and unclenched his hands, then wagged his boots. "I ain't gonna lose nothin', am I?"

"Only your life if you don't start talking," Shotgun Sallie growled.

"My uncle Wolf took the whores up to his ranch, which is about six miles outside of a little settlement named Clear Creek."

Shotgun Sallie lowered her gun. "Isn't that about thirty or thirty-five miles southwest of here?"

"That's right. Wolf has a ranch there and that's where he and the others took those pretty young whores."

"How do I know you're not lying?" Shotgun Sallie demanded. "At this point I think you'd say anything to save your sorry hide."

"I ain't lyin'!" Elmer cried. "I want to live, and anyway, I never liked nor had much to do with my uncle . . . until just recently."

Shotgun Sallie turned to Longarm. "Can we trust him?"

"I don't know."

"Then I have the solution. We'll load Elmer up in a buckboard and take him to Clear Creek. If his uncle and the others *aren't* there, then we'll hang his lyin' ass from a big aspen tree. So we're bringing a rope."

Elmer's eyes widened. "I sure don't want to hang. Please, don't hang me!"

"All right," Shotgun Sallie said agreeably, "you have my sworn oath that we won't hang you if you're telling us the truth."

"Shotgun," Longarm said, "I'm not altogether sure that his wounds won't reopen in a rough bouncing buckboard. He could bleed to death if we move him that far."

"That's a chance Elmer is going to have to take," she replied, turning away and holstering her gun. "Jesse!"

"Yes, ma'am?"

"We'll leave at first light."

The cowboy nodded and then Rabbit stepped forward and said, "I want to go, too."

"We *all* want to go," one of the women said. "We don't want to stay here and wait like we did tonight."

Longarm started to argue, but Shotgun Sallie said, "Fair enough. We'll take a pair of buckboards and all of you can come along to Clear Creek so long as you understand that we're going to fight."

"What about Bert?" one of the women asked.

"If he can stand the travel, he can come along lying beside Elmer here in one of the buckboards," Shotgun Sallie decided. "We're going to need all the help we can get when we get to Clear Creek, provided that's really where this Wolf Fernow and his men have taken my girls."

"Shotgun, are you dead sure about this?" Longarm asked, unable to imagine why they would want to take a bunch of old whores and fellas who had long since seen their better days. To his way of thinking, they would be far more trouble than they could possibly be worth.

"They did just fine after you tossed that string of firecrackers, didn't they?" Shotgun Sallie argued.

Longarm studied the old, lined faces and saw no fear. "You're right," he finally replied. "They did *better* than just fine. They did one hell of a job, and I expect that they've earned the right to come along for the showdown."

Everyone in the room lifted a little bit higher from Longarm's praise, and he had a feeling that not a single one of them was going to fold if the going got tough and bloody at Clear Creek.

Chapter 21

Longarm and his odd band of warriors had left the Shotgun Ranch at first light and traveled as fast as they could all day. They didn't come across a lot of travelers, but when they did they sure did get bizarre looks. They were composed of two buckboards, two seriously shot-to-shit men, five old whores, and Jesse the cowboy, along with himself and Shotgun Sallie. It didn't get any more outlandish than that, but Longarm had a good sense that everything was going to work out in their favor. The whores, Jesse, and even old Bert were determined to rescue Shotgun Sallie's three young whores, and they were just as determined to wipe the slate clean with the Fernow Clan once and for all.

Longarm was driving the buckboard that was transporting Bert and Elmer. Now, he yelled over his shoulder, "Elmer, how much farther to your uncle Wolf's ranch?"

The young man pushed himself up from the blanket he was lying on and gawked around for a minute, then said, "We're about three miles from Clear Creek. But my uncle's ranch has a cutoff that you can take and save some time and miles."

"How far to the cutoff and then how far to the ranch?" Shotgun Sallie demanded from the fine horse she was riding.

"It's about a mile to the cutoff and another four miles up a canyon to the ranch's boundary. Wolf's cabin is hidden back in a grove of trees and you don't see it until you're almost in his yard."

"That's what we needed to know," Longarm said, arching his stiff and aching back. He wished he'd been able to ride a good horse, but he was needed as a buckboard driver and Jesse was the only other one of them able to drive a four-horse team.

"Hey!" Bert cried. "I sure am thirsty! How about just a little taste of rotgut whiskey?"

"Nope," Shotgun Sallie told him. "As long as you're eatin' my food and sleepin' on my ranch, you're stayin' sober."

Bert raised and shook his fist at the sky. "I didn't say nothin' about gettin' drunk, dammit! And at the moment I sure ain't sleepin' on your ranch or eatin' your food. What I am is gettin' the shit shaken outa me!"

"Shut up and rest," Longarm said with a grin. "We want you to be able to handle a gun or rifle when we get to the Fernow place."

"I know, I know. But I could sure as hell shoot better with a steady hand, and the only way that I'll have that is if I get a little taste of the hair of the dog."

"Forget it," Shotgun Sallie told him.

"Damn," Bert swore, "that is a hard, hard woman."

Longarm was driving the lead wagon and made the turn when it came up. Jesse, skillfully driving the second buckboard carrying most of the old ex-whores, followed right along.

Shotgun Sallie rode up beside Longarm and asked,

"Custis, I don't think it's too much to ask if you have some sort of plan."

"Plan?"

"Yeah. And it really needs to be a plan that won't get my three best whores shot all to hell."

"I'm going to put some thought to that one right now," he promised.

"Well, Lawman, you'd better start thinking hard," Shotgun Sallie said, not looking in the least bit impressed. "Because we'll be at Wolf's cabin right about sundown."

Longarm frowned and started trying to put together some plan of action. After another mile, he decided that the best way to do this was simply to stop the wagons before they could be seen, then unload everyone and circle Wolf's lair. After that they'd come up with something.

They were going up a steep and narrow rutted road that wound its way beside a tiny creek. All the horses and people were thirsty, so Longarm pulled his buckboard up and everyone took turns getting a cold drink of the clear, cold mountain water.

"I'd be careful about how much of that I drank," Elmer Fernow advised, lifting up from his place in the buckboard.

"And why is that?" Rabbit demanded.

"'Cause my uncle and his kinfolks regularly shit and piss in that creek."

Water squirted out through Rabbit's buck teeth, and everyone else including Longarm suddenly decided that they weren't so thirsty after all.

"You should have told us that earlier, you little turd!" Jesse swore. "If I come down with the trots because of this water, I'm going to throttle you."

"Get in line, old man," Elmer said, lying back down on his blanket. "Lawman, you'd better get that plan in mind because Wolf's cabin ain't more'n half a mile ahead. Pretty quick, one of his dogs will hear or smell us comin' and set up a howl."

"How many men and how many dogs does Wolf own?"

"About a half dozen curs and about that many men, I reckon."

Longarm scuffed the creek gravel with the toe of his boot. Finally, he said, "Elmer, I reckon those dogs know you pretty well, huh?"

"They know me."

"Then I'm going to put you on a horse and you're going to ride up to your uncle's cabin and hail the Fernow men inside. When they come out, we'll all be in hiding and they'll either surrender or we'll cut them down where they stand."

Elmer shook his head. "What you're askin' me to do is commit suicide and I won't do that. If I ride in there alone, I'm a dead man."

Shotgun Sallie said, "He's right, but I don't care a hoot about him. It's my young whores that count. Maybe . . ." Her words trailed off.

"What?" Longarm asked.

"Maybe I'll ride in there with Elmer. In the poor light, they'll assume that I'm one of the ones that survived the shoot-out in my ranch yard. They'll let me ride up real close to the cabin and I'll yank my shotgun out from under my coat and open up with both barrels."

"That's the worst plan I've ever heard," Longarm told her.

"Have you got a better one?"

"No."

"Then that's what I'm going to do," Shotgun Sallie said with conviction. "It'll happen fast and it's my best chance to get in close range for the shotgun."

"It's no chance for you at all."

"I disagree, and since I'm responsible for those three girls, I'm doing this my way."

Longarm gave it a moment of thought and then nodded his head. "All right. It's your call, Shotgun."

"Good," she said, looking surprised. "I was sure you'd give me a big argument and there's no time now for that."

"You're absolutely right," Longarm said. "I'll unhitch one of the horses for Elmer to ride in bareback."

"I ain't gettin' on any damned horse!" the young Fernow cried in protest. "I ain't leavin' this wagon!"

Longarm jumped down from the wagon, clamped his hand over Elmer's mouth, and jammed his pistol into the young man's leg . . . the one that had been shot. Elmer would have howled, but Longarm's hand cut that down to a whimper.

"You ready to ride, or shall I get out my knife and start cutting?" Longarm asked the kid.

"I'll ride!" Elmer gasped. "But when my uncle comes out, I'm gonna skedaddle as fast as I can. Wolf ain't gonna surrender and neither are the others."

"Just get Shotgun Sallie in close," Longarm ordered. "That's all that you have to do and then you can get the hell out of the way."

"Okay," Elmer said, his voice shaky. "I'll do it."

"Glad to hear that," Longarm told him. "Shotgun, you need to get down from that horse and come over here and take a peek at Bert. He ain't lookin' too healthy."

Shotgun Sallie dismounted and came over to the buckboard. She peered in at the old cowboy and said, "Are you still alive, Bert?"

"Hell, yes! And I want a pistol! I ain't about to lie here while all the rest of you get to have the fun."

"Here's an extra one I brought along," Shotgun Sallie said, reaching into her waistband and drawing out a gun.

"Mind if I see that before you give it to Bert?" Longarm asked.

"Why?"

"I just want to make sure that it's in good working order."

Shotgun Sallie wasn't too happy but she handed the gun to Longarm. "That Colt is fine and . . ."

In a swift, totally unexpected move, Longarm palmed the extended weapon and then swung it in a tight half circle. The barrel of the Colt revolver cracked against the side of Shotgun Sallie's head and she dropped like a rock.

"Hey!" Bert shouted, trying to rise up from the buckboard. "What the hell did you do that for?"

Longarm reached inside Shotgun Sallie's coat and removed her beloved weapon. "Because *I'm* going to ride in with Elmer and open fire on Wolf and his bunch."

Everyone was in shock and clearly upset by what he had done, but Longarm knew he was doing the right thing. He didn't know if Wolf had been one of the ones who had killed poor Lucy Coyle while she was picnicking with him beside the South Platte River, but he probably had been. No matter now, because Longarm had his own burning revenge to satisfy and a bloody debt to be paid.

Starting and ending tonight.

"You might have hurt her real bad," one of the old whores said accusingly. "You didn't have to hit her that way."

"Yes, I did," Longarm said. "Let's get her laid out in the buckboard. You and the others who really want a part of this fight stay here and get ready to come in when the shooting starts."

* * *

Less than five minutes later with Elmer riding bareback all slumped over and barely able to stay on a horse, Longarm trailed the young man up the dirt road and into the trees.

"You think we have any chance at all," Elmer said weakly. "I sure don't want to die tonight."

"Me, neither."

"But we're probably gonna."

"Yep," Longarm agreed as if he didn't have a care in the world.

"Ain't there any better way than this?"

"Not that I can think of." He was about to tell the young Fernow man that in this semidarkness he did stand at least a fifty-fifty chance of riding off with his life. But suddenly, Wolf Fernow's dogs started barking.

"Here we go," Longarm said. "Just get me up close to Wolf and then get out of my way."

"You don't need to tell me that," Elmer said, his voice a high, shaky whisper. "I'm already as good as gone."

Chapter 22

There was smoke coming out of Wolf's chimney and a couple of men on the porch drinking and laughing when the dogs sounded their loud warning. Suddenly, everyone on the porch and in the cabin piled outside. Two men came out with their pants down around their knees and Longarm had no trouble guessing what they'd been up to moments earlier. He just hoped that Shotgun Sallie's three whores were smart enough to dive for cover when the bullets began to fly.

"Who goes there!" a man shouted, raising his rifle.

"You'd better answer your kin or we're dead men," Longarm hissed.

"It's me, Elmer!"

"Elmer?"

"Sure, Uncle Wolf. Don't shoot. I've already been wounded."

"And who is that ridin' beside you," Wolf shouted as the riders kept coming closer. "Is that you, Mort?"

"Yep!" Longarm called out in the failing light as his hand unbuttoned his coat and his finger closed loosely on the shotgun's trigger.

"Well, come on in, boys! We thought you two were shot dead at that woman's ranch."

"Nope," Longarm called, making his voice sound rough. "But we're hurt some."

Wolf Fernow lowered his rifle and approached to help them. When he was within twenty feet he seemed to realize that Longarm was not Mort, and as he raised his rifle, Longarm dropped the shotgun on him and said, "Don't do it, Wolf."

"What the . . . ?"

Longarm knew by the way that Wolf Fernow tensed and spoke that he had no intention of surrendering. And as Wolf's rifle started to come to the level, Longarm squeezed the trigger of his shotgun.

The explosion sounded like that of a heavy Civil War cannon. Wolf was a big man, but when he took the blast he lifted off the ground and was hurled backward toward his cabin. Longarm knew the leader of the Fernow Clan was dead even before he skidded into the side of his cabin.

Elmer kicked his horse and shot off at an angle, yelling, "Kill him, boys! He's not Mort, he's a gawdamn lawman!"

Longarm swung the shotgun and fired again and a man disappeared as if he'd been yanked by a wire back through the cabin door. Longarm tossed the heavy weapon aside and made a grab for his gun, but the fine Morgan he was riding started bucking and Longarm found himself clawing at the stars.

Gunfire erupted as if they were on a battlefield, and when Longarm struck the ground he rolled and kept rolling until he ended up behind a water trough.

He'd bruised his left shoulder but that didn't keep him from returning fire, then getting to his feet and charging the cabin. He dimly realized he'd been nicked someplace but he just kept running. When Longarm reached the open cabin door, his gun was blazing.

There were screams from the whores inside and some-one was emptying a pistol as fast as a trigger could be pulled. A Fernow man staggered into Longarm's path, eyes glazing as he tried to reach back behind to plug the bullet hole in his spine. Longarm shot him in the forehead and then he stumbled over another man's body and fell.

A woman's wild scream split the room and Longarm glanced up to see a crazy-eyed whore launch herself at one of the last standing Fernow men with a butcher knife. The man was so terrified he dropped his gun and took the knife thrust to his stomach.

Longarm saw the woman stab the fallen man again and again and it was a sight that he knew he would not soon forget. Another whore jumped on the back of a completely naked man trying to crawl under a bed. She expertly grabbed his hair, pulled his head back, and slit his throat.

It was over.

Longarm must have lost consciousness for a short time because when it returned he was lying on a dirty mattress with Shotgun Sallie at his side.

"Hello?" was all he could think of to say.

"Hello, hell! You knocked me out and took my shot-gun!"

"Sorry, but it was the plan I came up with when you made it plain that you weren't going to let me ride in with Elmer."

"Elmer came racing past all of us like his ass was on fire."

"Did you shoot him?"

"I didn't. Jesse did. He probably would have died of blood loss anyway."

"That's right. Elmer was the last of the Fernow men."

"I sure hope so," Shotgun Sallie told him. "My girls are safe, but they were treated real badly by this bunch. I found six bottles of whiskey here and we're all getting drunk."

"What about Bert Hollister?"

Shotgun Sallie tilted her head a little to one side. "Bert has been through hell and I have always believed that rules are meant to be broken."

Longarm shook his head. "So you let that old sot have a drink?"

"Just one. A small one. He isn't happy about that, but things are tough all over, don't you think?"

"I sure do. Are you gonna stay mad at me for a while, Shotgun?"

"How could I do that after you saved my girls and almost single-handedly killed all those Fernow bastards?"

"Your whores helped."

"Yeah, I know that. And that's why we're all getting drunk and then tomorrow morning we're going to bury the dead and get on back to the ranch."

Longarm looked at the bandage on his arm. "I'm not feeling real good, Shotgun."

She touched the big lump on her pretty head where he'd beaned her a good one. "Neither am I. Neither are any of us, and that's why we mean to build a bonfire out of this cabin and get drunk watching it burn."

"If you're going to do that I ought to get off this bed and get out there and get drunk with you," Longarm decided.

Shotgun Sallie leaned over and kissed his mouth. "Come on, Big Boy," she said. "I'll help you, and then we'll share one of those bottles."

"I'd like that," he said, not wanting to look at all the blood that had pooled on the rough wooden floor. "Sounds like one hell of a good plan to me."

"Someone has to do the planning around here," she told him as they stepped over a body and passed out into the sweet mountain air. "And I'm sure as hell not leaving that up to you anymore."

Longarm didn't feel up to an argument with Shotgun Sallie. Besides, he rather liked the idea of getting drunk and burning Wolf Fernow's stinking cabin right down to the ground.

GIANT-SIZED ADVENTURE FROM
AVENGING ANGEL LONGARM.

BY TABOR EVANS

2006 Giant Edition:

**LONGARM AND THE
OUTLAW EMPRESS**

2007 Giant Edition:

**LONGARM AND THE
GOLDEN EAGLE SHOOT-OUT**

2008 Giant Edition:

**LONGARM AND THE
VALLEY OF SKULLS**

2009 Giant Edition:

**LONGARM AND THE
LONE STAR TRACKDOWN**

penguin.com/actionwesterns

M456AS0409

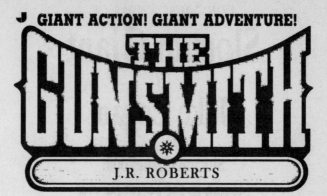

GIANT ACTION! GIANT ADVENTURE!

THE Gunsmith

J.R. ROBERTS

penguin.com/actionwesterns

M455AS0509